Jamaal Lee

UrbanLee Vibrant
jamaal.lee4@yahoo.com
www.jamaallee.com

Dedicated to Howard J. & Mary H. Lee

Story Arc 1

A boy named Zion lives on the planet Solar Moon. The planet's population consists of aliens, creatures, and humanoids. Scratch, Zion's best friend, is a hybrid of both human and cat. Zion and Scratch are in their fourth-period classroom when they receive their graded assignments from Ms. Beetle, whom the boys detest.

She is an actual beetle. The bell rings for lunchtime. Dissatisfied with their final grades, both boys plan a prank for Ms. Beetle for grading them unfairly.

After the boys set up their prank, Zion will lure Ms. Beetle into the hallway, where there is slippery goo on the floor and a surprising set done by Scratch. Before he can carry out his intentions, Ms. Beetle asks for a word with Zion.

She has him sit and discusses her concerns. She informs him that she doesn't despise him at all but only expects the best from him. She returns his assignment again with a fairer grade.

With gratitude, Zion has a change of heart about Ms. Beetle. Acknowledging his faults and behavior lately, Zion promises to do better not only for his grades but for himself too. Delighted, Ms. Beetle asks Zion to come with her to the cafeteria get a soda.

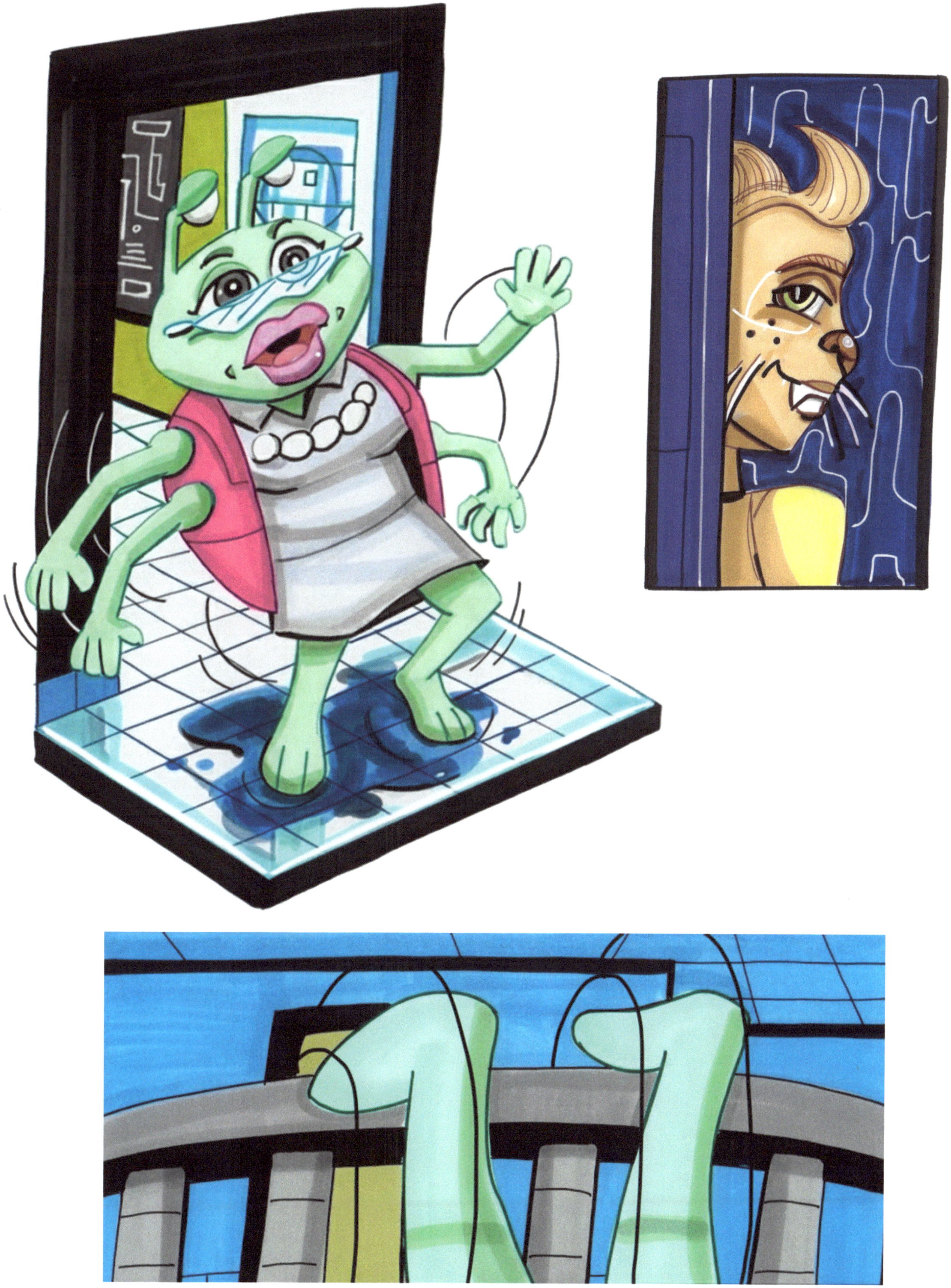

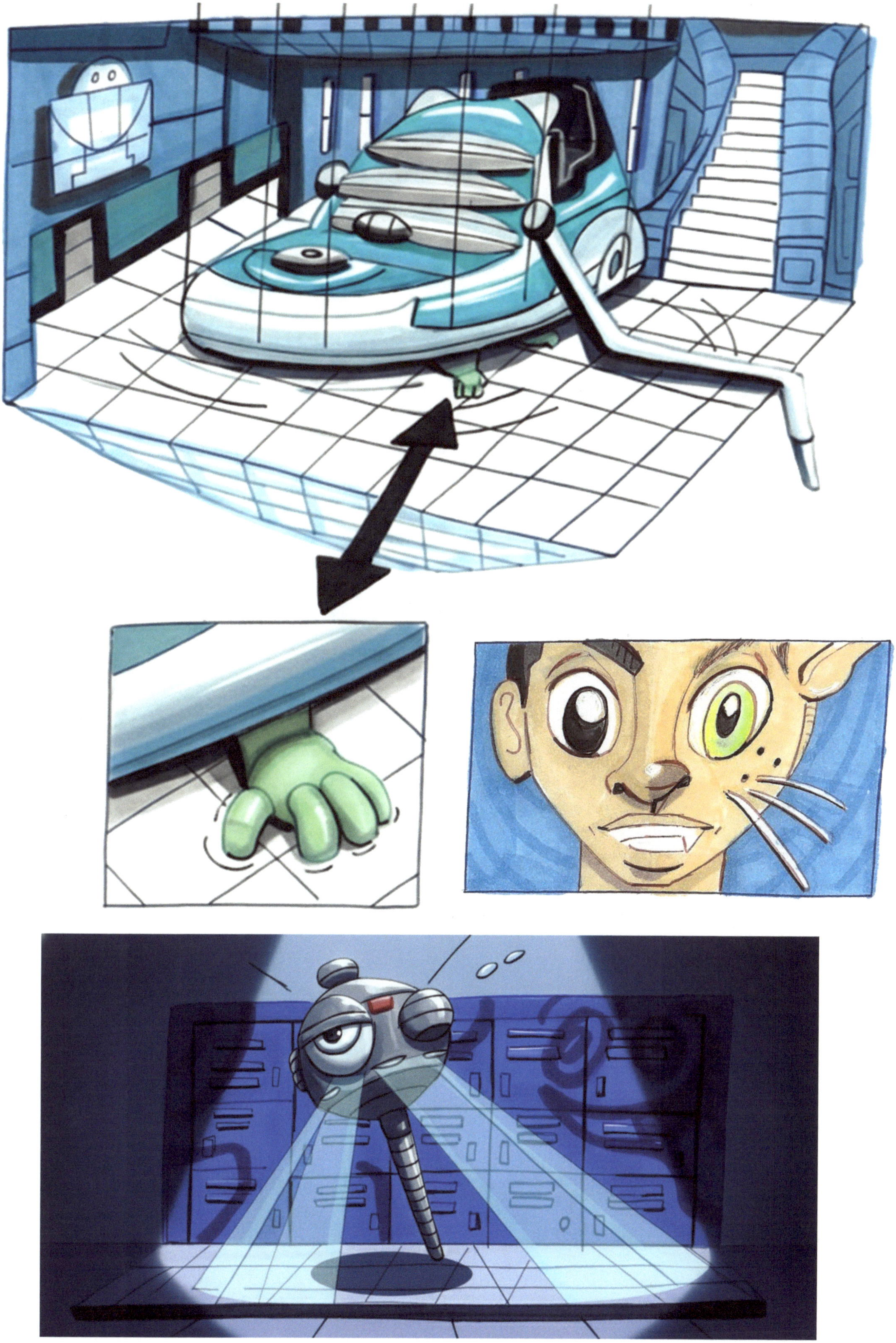

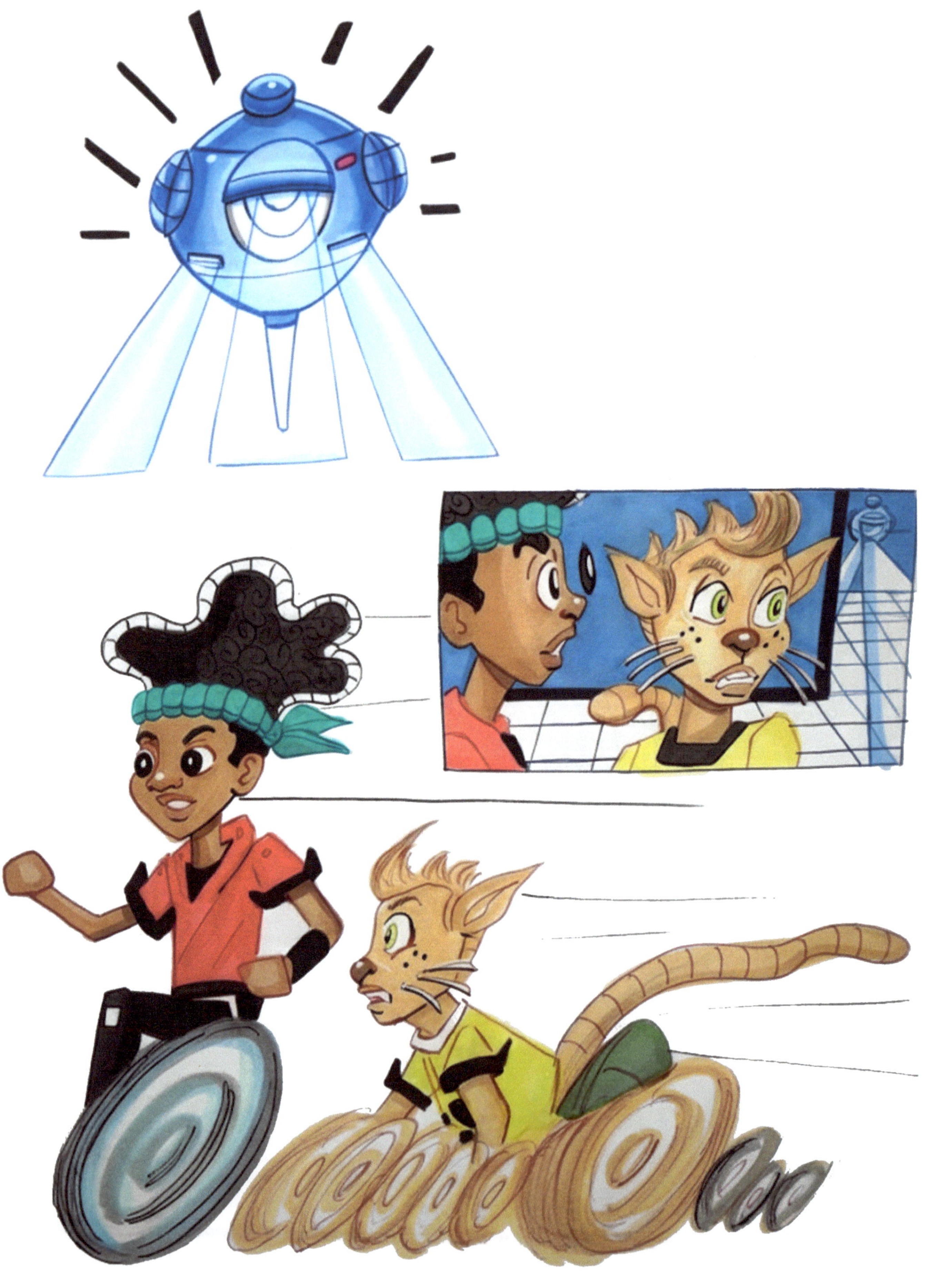

Forgetting the slippery floor, Zion fails to inform Ms. Beetle before walking into the hallway. Unaware, Ms. Beetle slips down the second-floor staircase. Scratch then releases a rope, lowering a large object revealing to be a dress shoe, from the ceiling, which falls onto Ms. Beetle. Both watch in alarm as they notice one of Ms. Beetle's legs is still moving. Frightened, they run away as the Hall Monitor approaches.

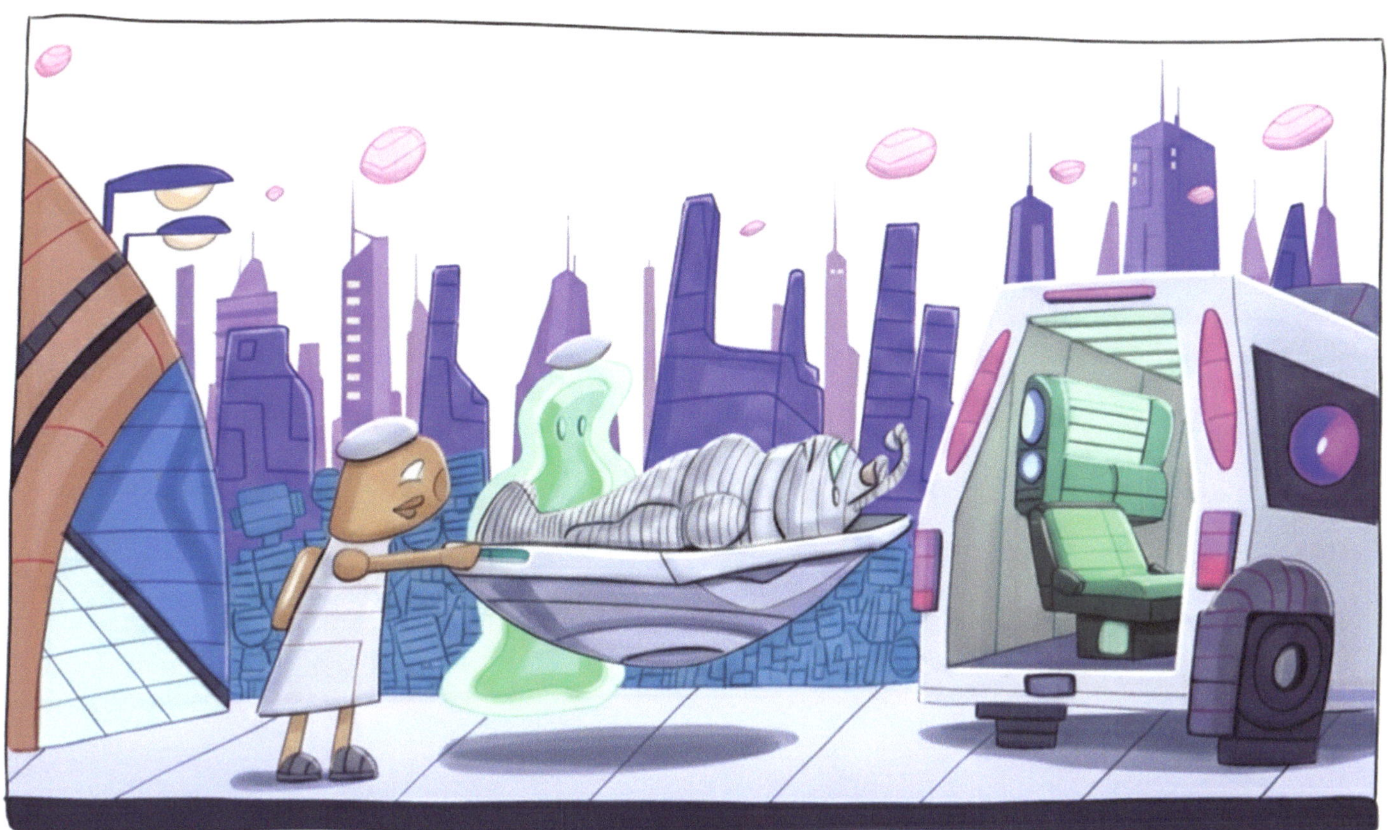

An hour later, Ms. Beetle, all wrapped up like a mummy due to her injuries, is loaded into an ambulance, which will transport her to Solar University Hospital. Principal Wildcat is furious. Over the loudspeaker, he vows to find the students responsible for Ms. Beetle's condition.

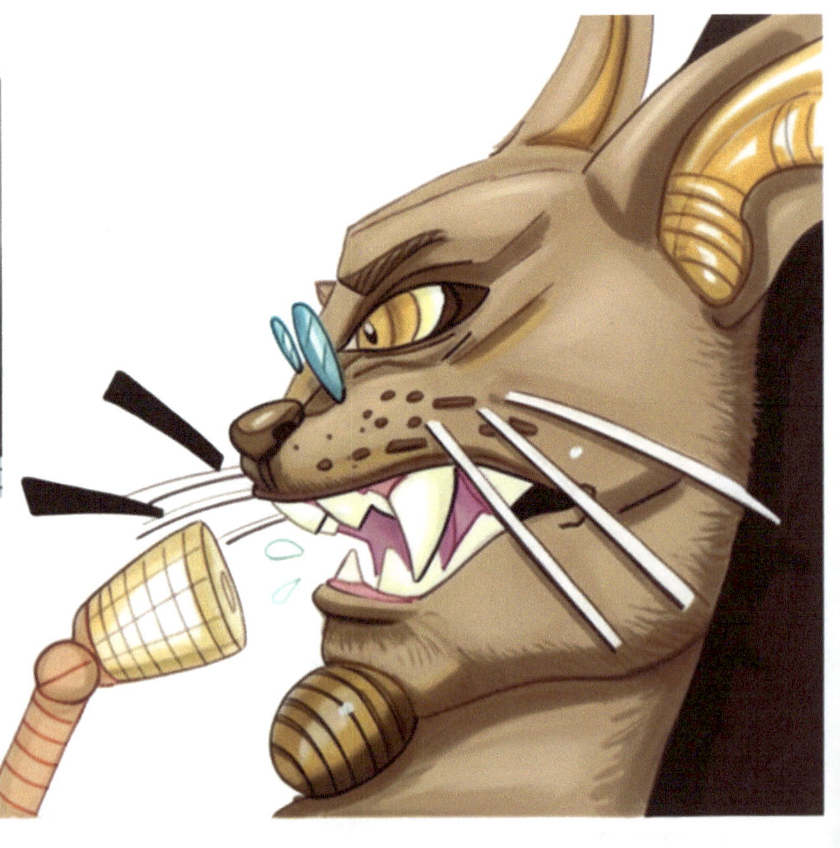

Hiding outside in the bushes near the ambulance, Zion and Scratch are contemplating how to frame the incident as an accident to Principal Wildcat. Unable to make logical sense out of the matter, they instead decide to skip school.

While walking home, Scratch insists they chill downtown at the harbor, their favorite spot to hide out, till things blow over.

Zion agrees as he walks into the apartment complex.

Inside, Zion notices his mother isn't home from work yet. Walking toward his bedroom, Zion notices a family portrait, a picture of a younger Zion with both his parents, on the living room shelf. As he picks up the portrait, he sadly stares at his father, wondering about his whereabouts and whatever happened to him seven years ago.

Five-year-old Zion is pretending to fly a space car on the shoulders of his father, Jeru. They begin to play a game of Space Cadets. Supper is ready, Zion's mother, Mary, calls them in for dinner.

As they finish saying grace for their meal, the doorbell rings. Mary returns to the kitchen and tells Jeru he has a visitor.

Curious, Zion creeps into the living room, hiding behind a door while eavesdropping. He looks over the door and sees a Pig-Man dressed in military armor.

It seems he is recruiting Jeru against his will to assist in the Battle Against Worlds. Jeru is irritated over the unlawful system decision that selected him, as he has a family of his own now since Earth's demise. The Pig-Man advises him that failure to assist will result in repercussions.

Later that evening, Zion is preparing for bedtime. He starts to hear his parents arguing.

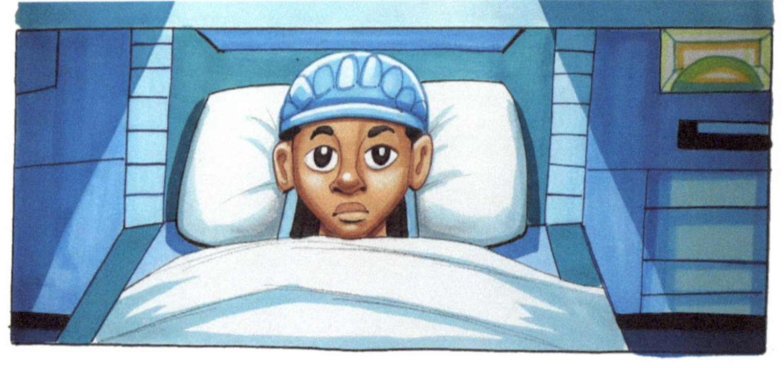

Jeru enters Zion's room to tuck him in, assuring him that, no matter what happens, he'll always be by his side.

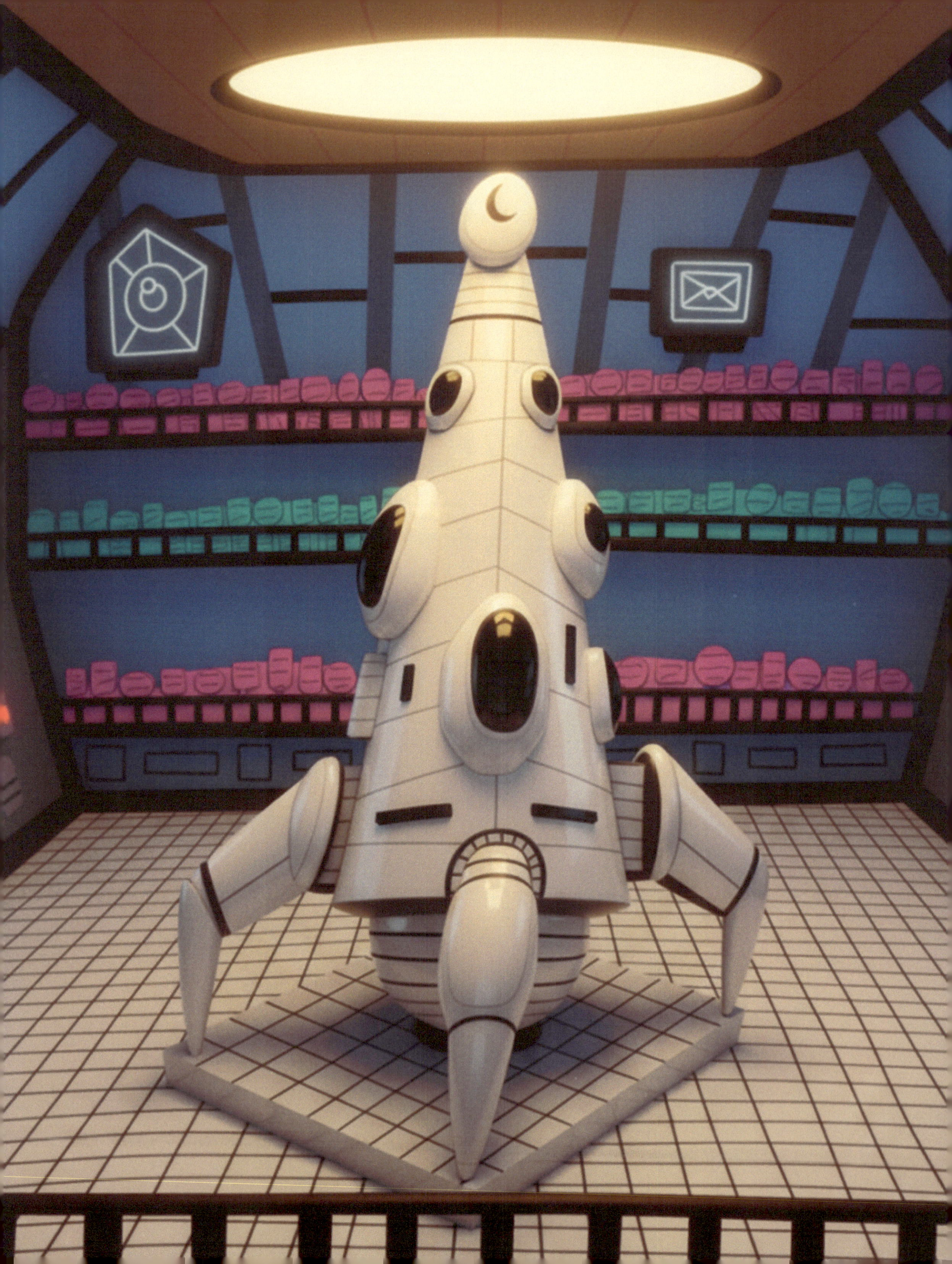

The day has finally come to assist in the ongoing Battle Against Worlds at the military base. All soldiers are equipping themselves. Before they are to launch into space, Jeru asks to speak with Mary and Zion privately. He shares a sweet kiss and hug with a teary-eyed Mary. Zion begs his father to stay and begins sobbing that he can't leave.

Jeru reassures Zion that he'll hardly know his father is gone and he will return in no time. He embraces Zion, telling him he loves him and instructing him to take good care of his mother. The general announces they'll be departing immediately, and all the soldiers board the spacecraft.

Jeru turns back to see Zion and then salutes him. Zion does the same. As the countdown reaches zero, the craft shoots up into the sky like a distant star. Families and supporters begin to applaud the soldiers, wishing them farewell in hopes of ending the war. While Zion stares into the sky, Mary hugs him as he starts to cry.

Remembering that day when he had last seen his father, Zion believes wholeheartedly that his father will return someday.

Arc 11

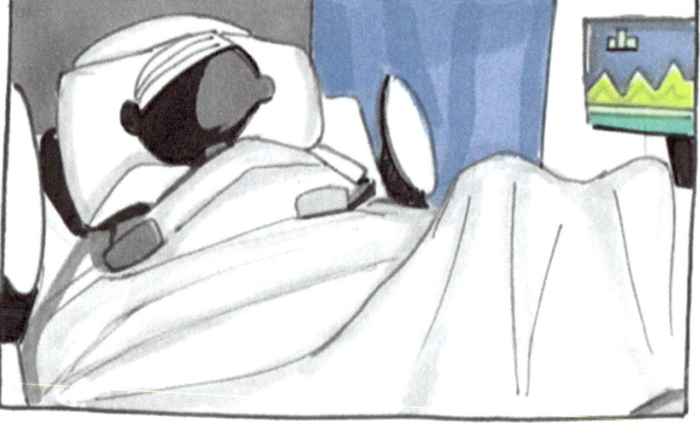

One Year Ago

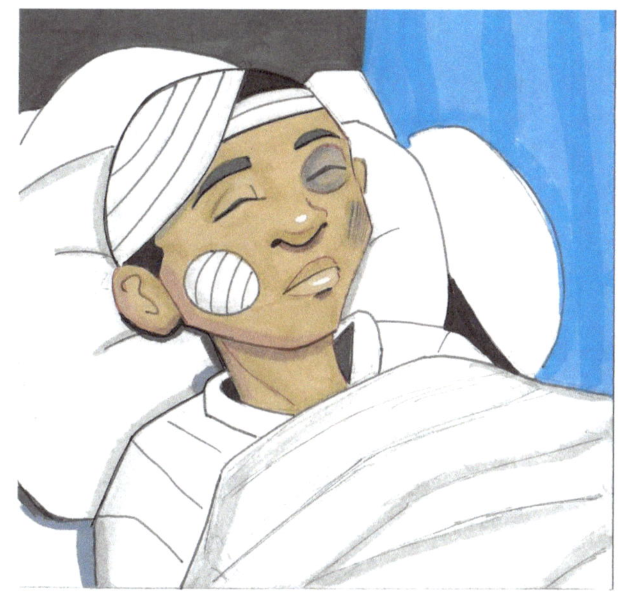

At Solar University Hospital, an unknown child has been under a coma for approximately two weeks after surviving a near-fatal accident. A friend, Zorrie, and her grandmother visit the boy. They have been staying by his bedside since the horrible accident and praying he regains consciousness before they pull his life support.

The doctors have warned that it's only a matter of time before he's declared brain-dead. A teary-eyed Zorrie warmly holds the young boy's hand. Slowly the young boy begins grasping his bedsheets. He opens his eyes. Zorrie and her grandmother both rejoice.

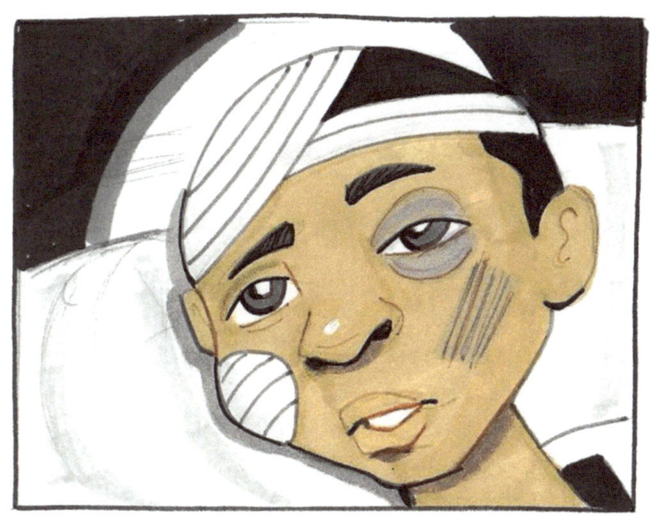

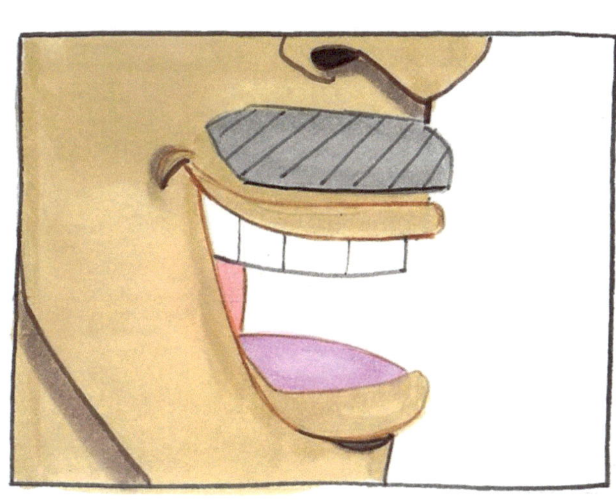

The boy begins to ask questions and requests to see his parents too. Sorrowful, Zorrie looks at the boy, but before she can answer his question, a tall man walks into the room and interrupts her.

He informs them that he is a psychologist, Dr. Mathlow. He will be helping the boy through his rehabilitation. He tells them all visiting hours are unfortunately over. Zorrie and her grandmother say their good-byes to the boy and state that they hope to see him again. Dr. Mathlow then begins to ask the young man if he remembers anything, such as his name.

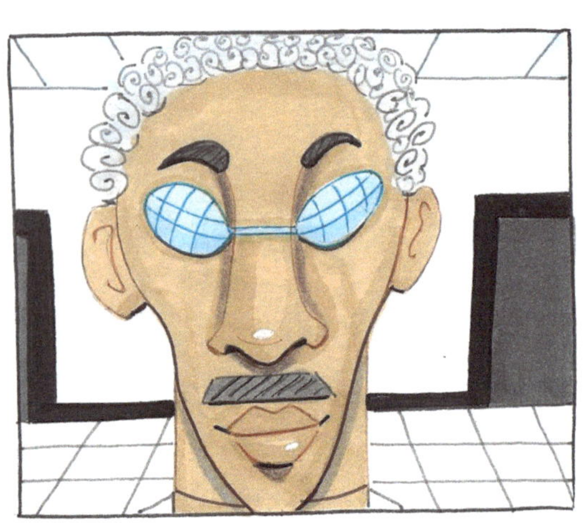

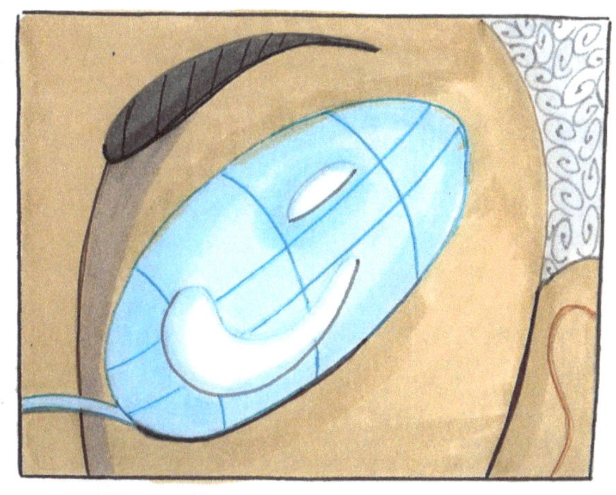

Unable to recall anything before being in the hospital, the young boy says, "Yates." He isn't sure whether that's his name or not, but he remembers Yates. The doctor says he will be called Yates for the time being. Dr. Mathlow suggests Yates is suffering from amnesia.

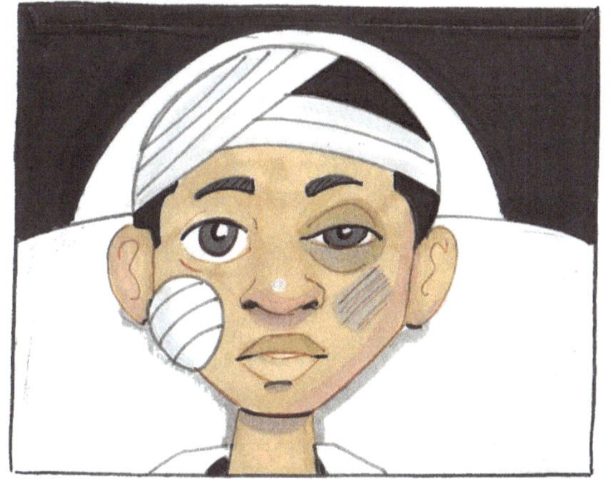

Wondering where his parents are, Yates questions their whereabouts. Dr. Mathlow then shares the tragic news: they died in the accident.

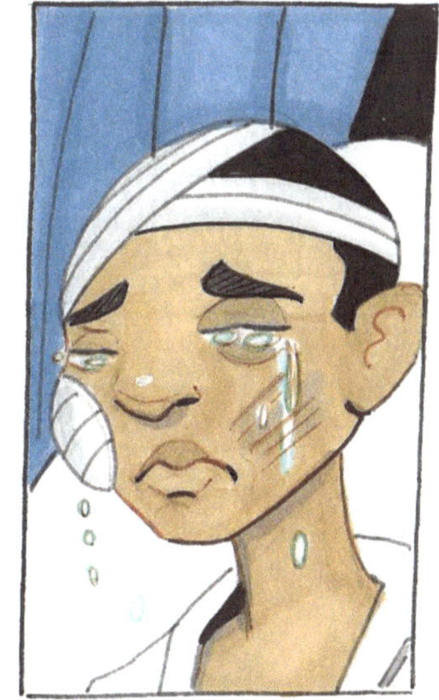

This upsetting news causes Yates to cry uncontrollably. Dr. Mathlow prepares a needle to help Yates sleep, but before injecting him, he states, "You, my son, a new life ahead awaits you."

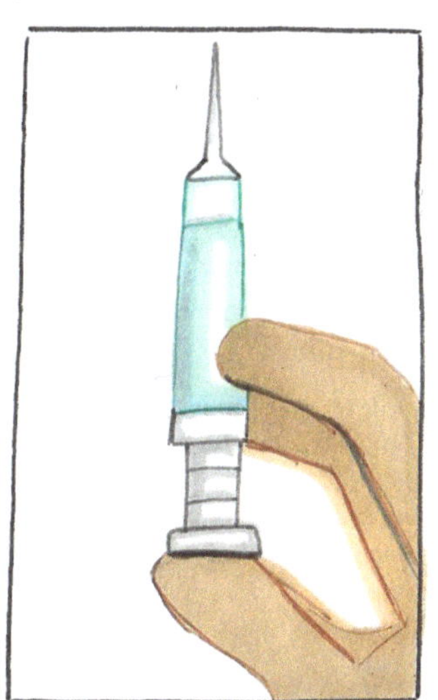

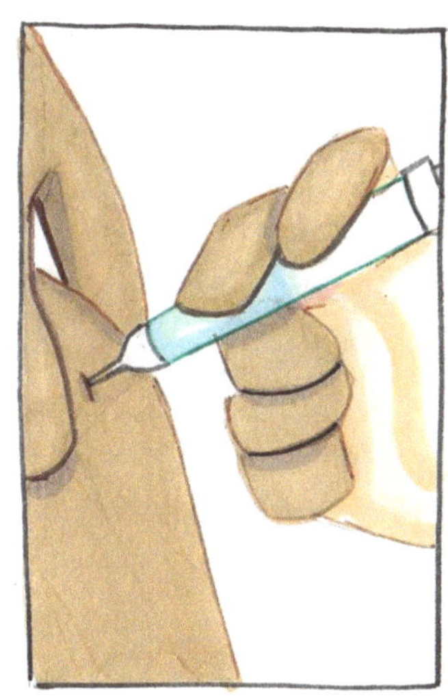

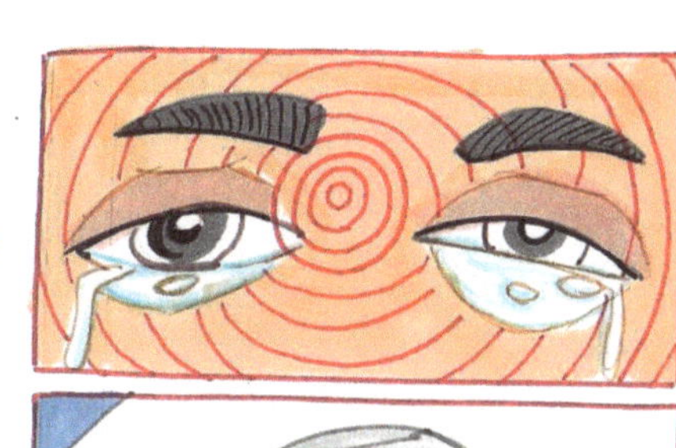

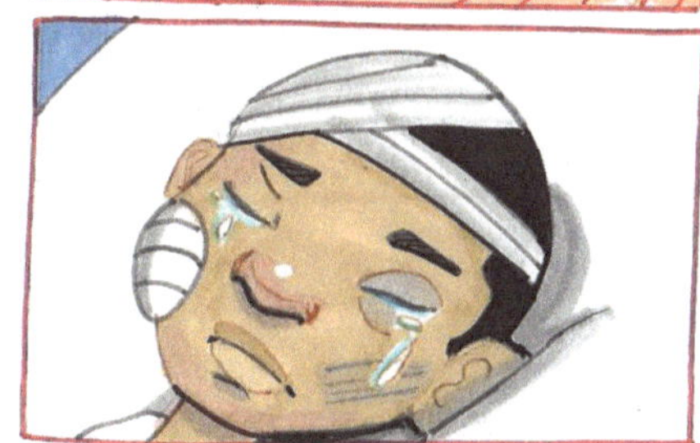

Later that evening, Dr. Mathlow attended a meeting with a leadership organization, the Nefarious, discussing their new department of human relations, which experiments on humans to turn them into artificial beings in support of a new order of life. Dr. Raheem believes they can rule Solar Moon and the entire galaxy with artificial intelligence drones at their command once they discover a way of taking human emotions away from them.

Dr. Mathlow, however, is not impressed. He states he would not participate in the action of risking more innocent lives as lab rats in a selfish ploy to rule the entire universe. The head of the organization agrees with Dr. Mathlow's perspective and asks that he continue his work with different methods. He vows he has a better alternative in shaping the entire

universe peacefully without destroying lives of all God's creations, to which each leader, except Dr. Raheem, applauds him.

Dr. Mathlow proclaims his new experiment, Yates, will be the solution to their problem. As Dr. Mathlow exits the meeting, Dr. Raheem murmurs that he'll get him back for that.

That same night, Dr. Mathlow returns to the hospital, only this time to his laboratory, to carry out his plan to transform Yates into an artificial bot. He removes Yates's heart and brain from his human body to be placed into the artificial body armor.

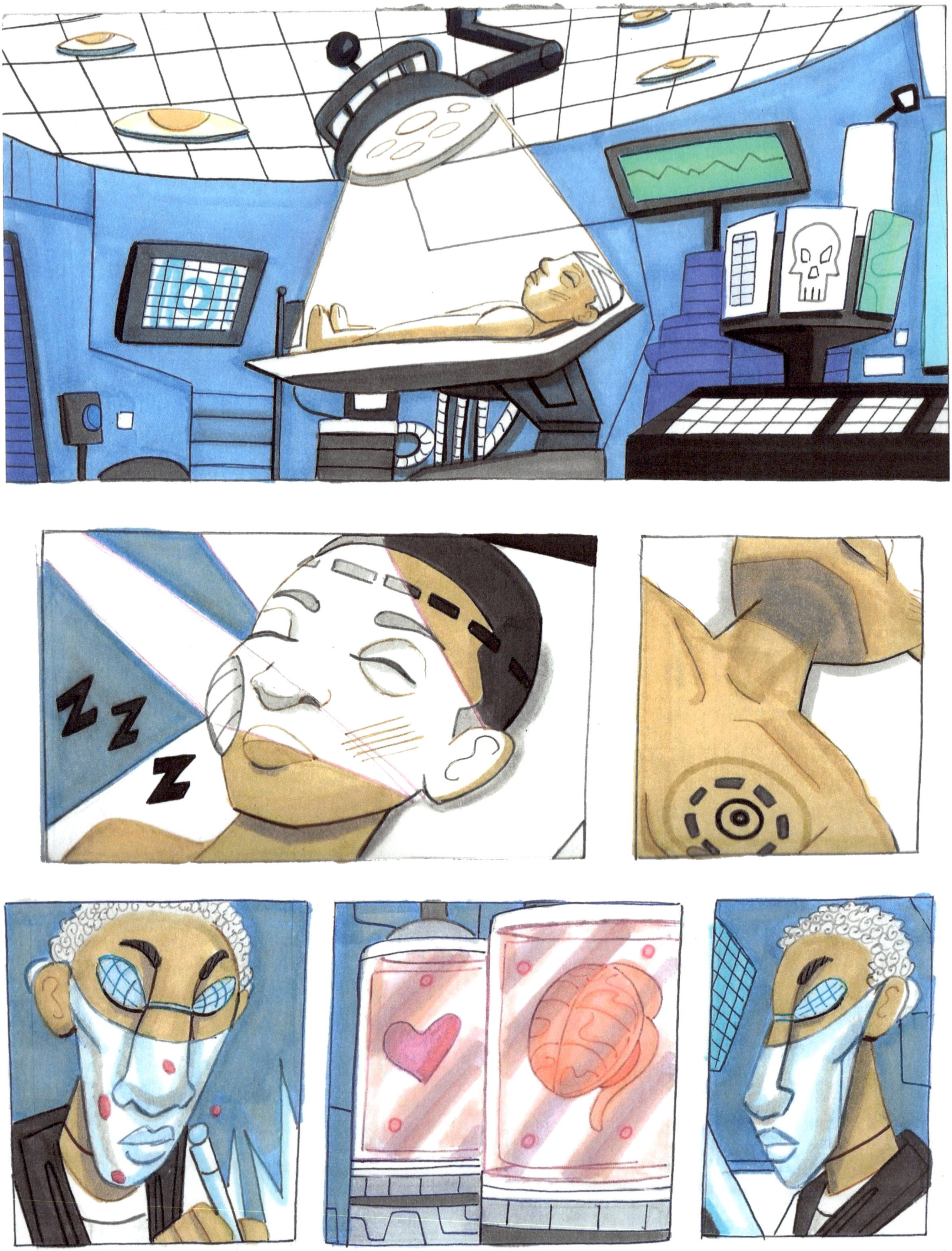

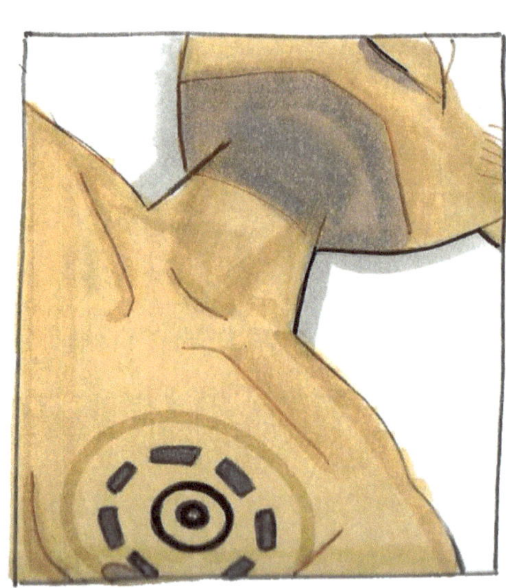

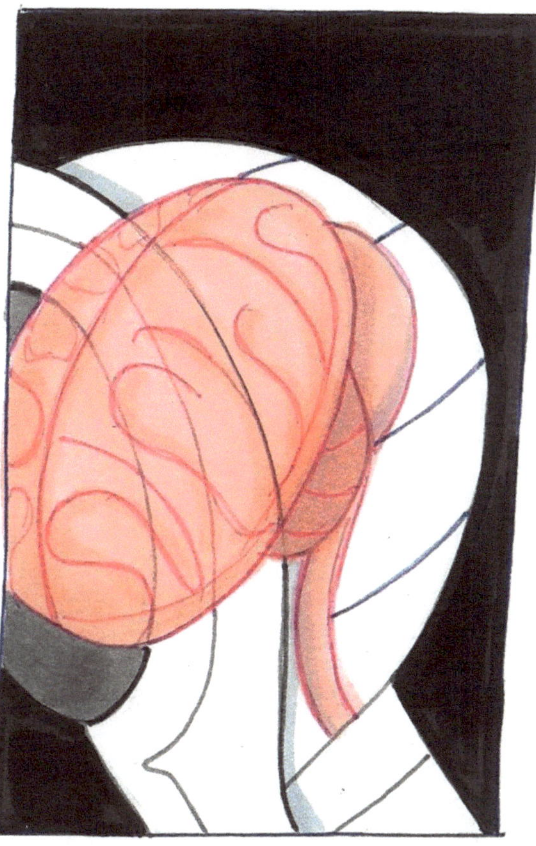

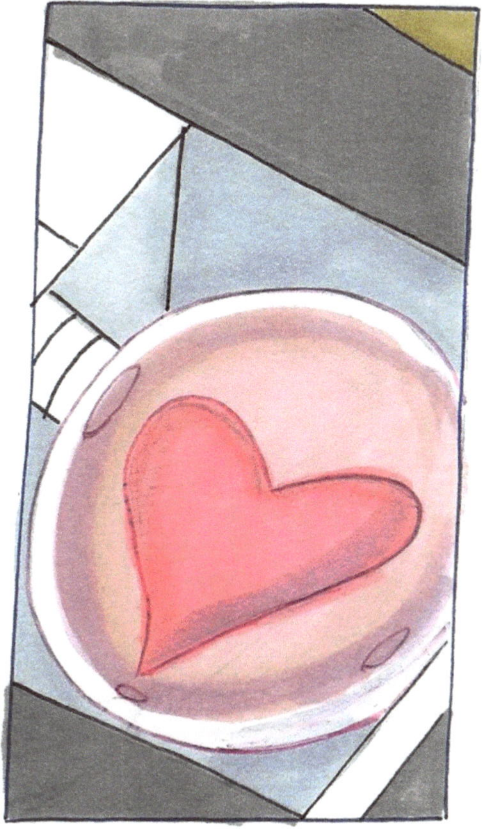

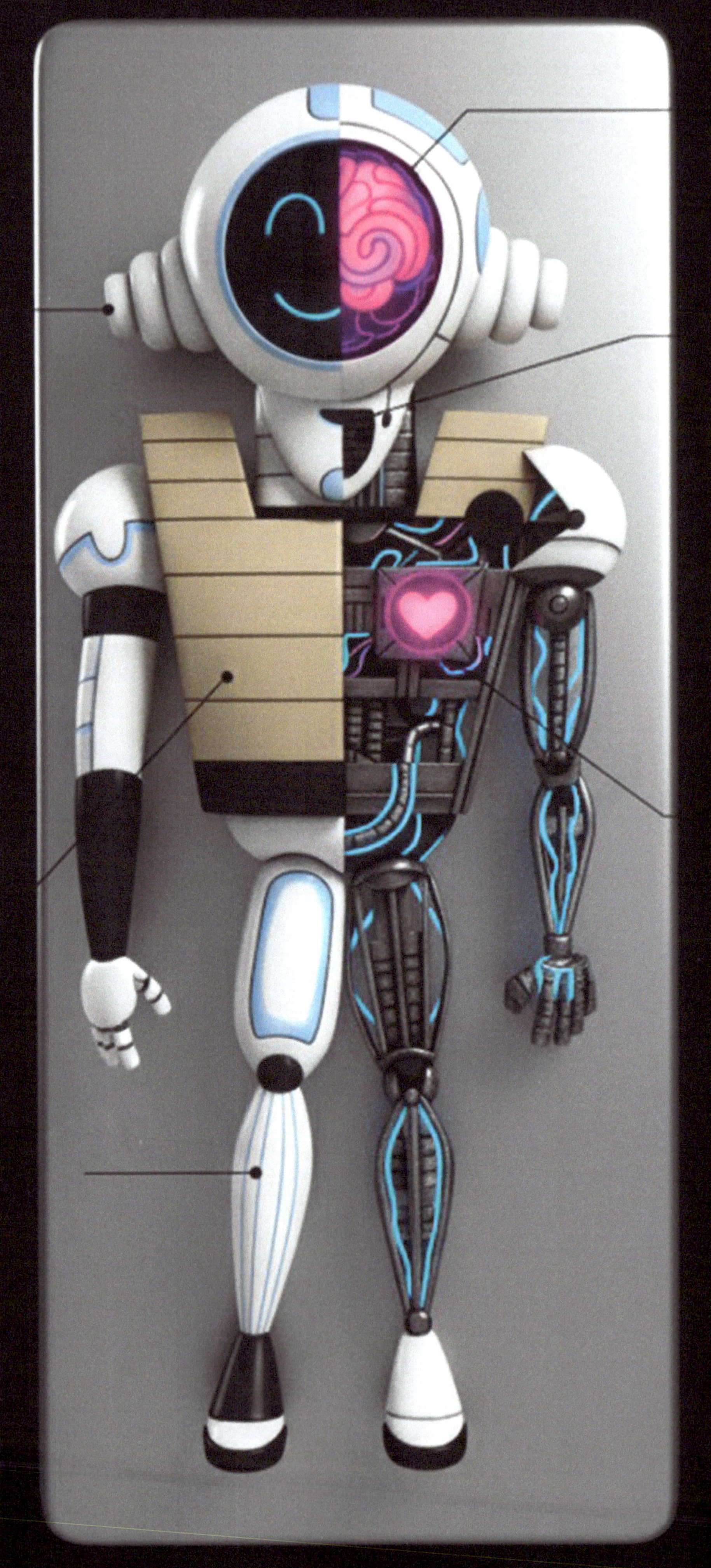

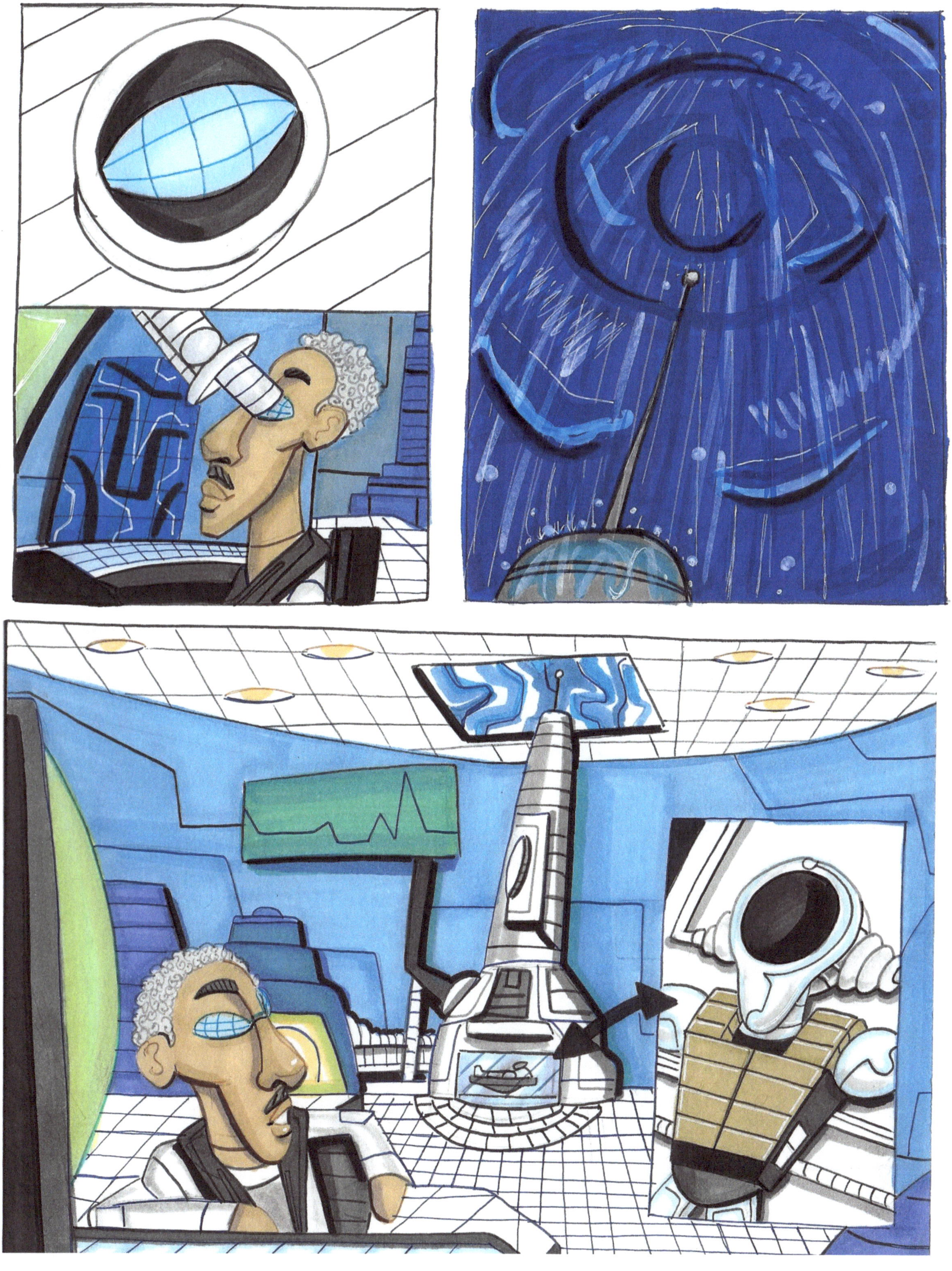

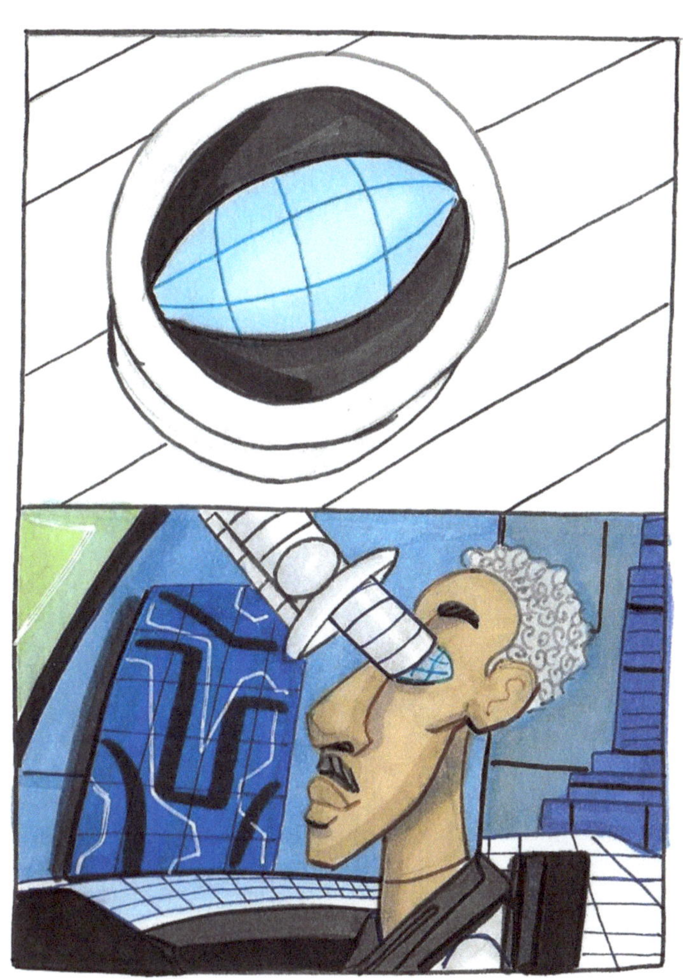

To make sure Yates is reincarnated with eternal life, Dr. Mathlow uses a rare atom he collected during his space journey to a deep hole within the farthest galaxy.

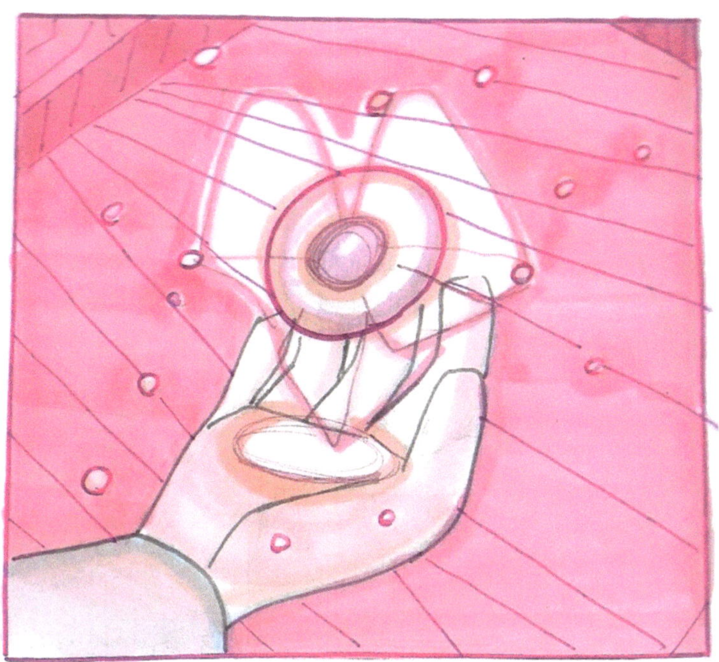

However, before he can bring Yates back to life, he must use a towering pole that will attract high bolts of electric lightning from a space storm.

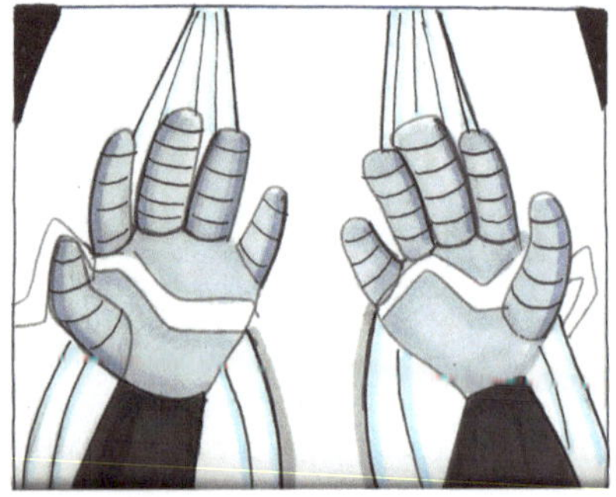

Securing the power source from the lightning strike, he loads the energy wave into Yates, causing an explosion. Unharmed, Dr. Mathlow shouts for Yates but hears no response from the motionless boy. Upset this might have been a mistake or failure, suddenly Yates's hands begin to move along with his sensors, proclaiming activation.

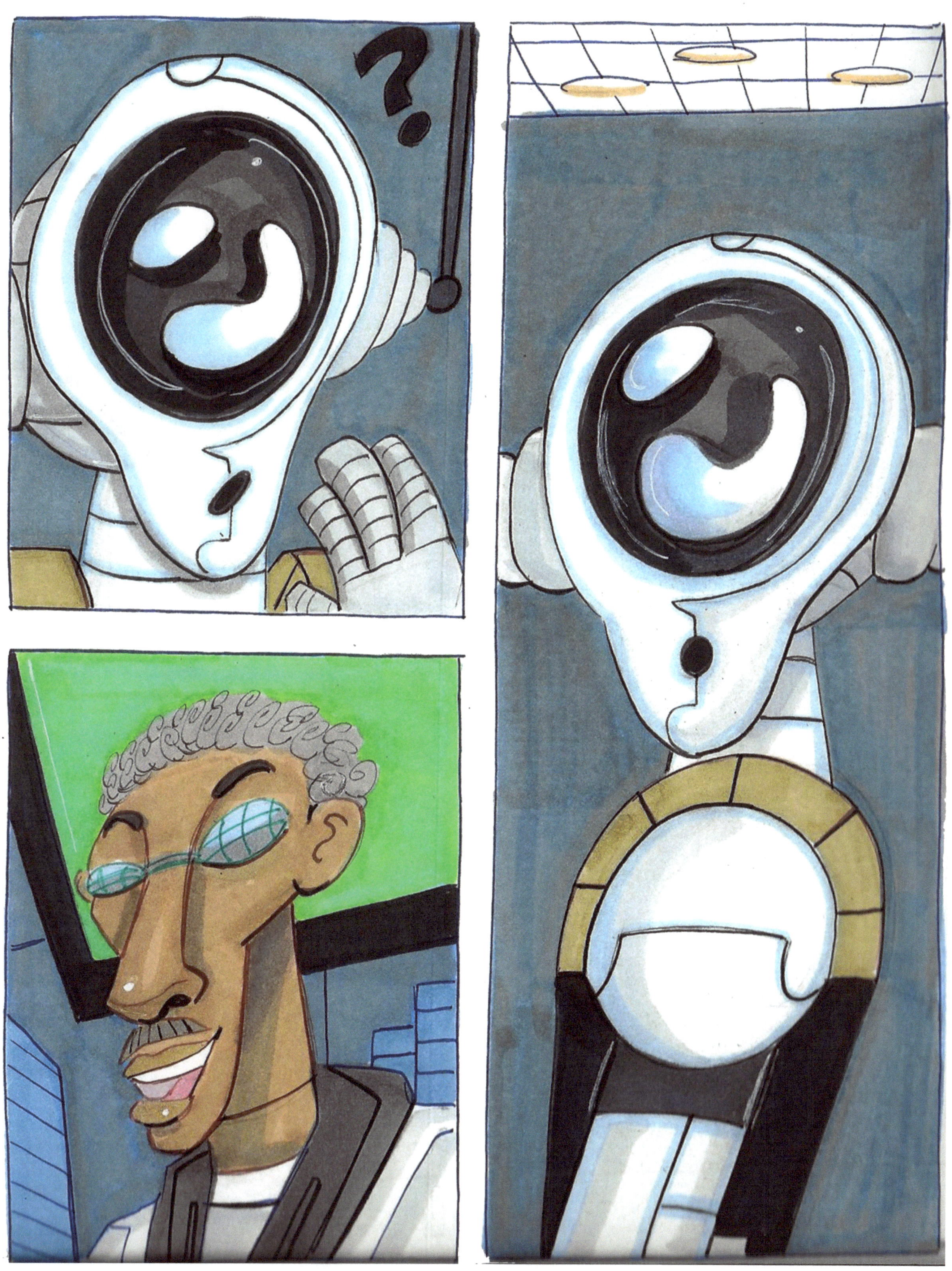

Dr. Mathlow is joyful Yates is alive and active. Yates begins to regain his memory, with him last being at the hospital. He's still sad that his parents are deceased, and Dr. Mathlow comforts him with the idea of living his life for the purpose of bringing joy to everyone and points out how amazing he is now, while looking in the mirror at his new artificial body.

Dr. Mathlow takes Yates in to live with him as his new guardian, as he will also study his special abilities. On the ride to his manor, Dr. Mathlow promises Yates a new life full of great things that'll come to him soon. Arriving at the home, Yates is introduced to Dr. Mathlow's two sons, Darius and Rile. They are robots too, although dissimilar to Yates: they are half-human and half-robotic. Nonetheless, Rile immediately accepts Yates into the family home as a new brother, whereas unfortunately Darius rejects Yates's welcome.

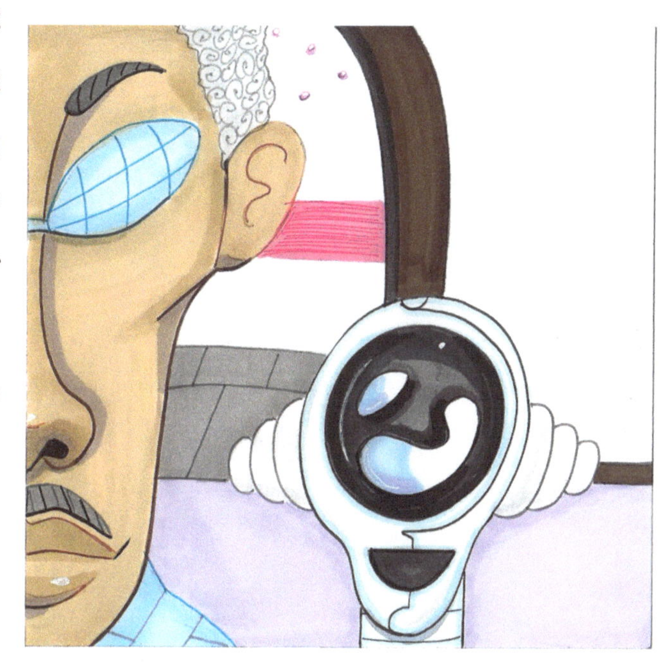

When Rile determines it'll be a while until Darius accepts Yates into the family home, he takes Yates into their game room. After playing a few games, he asks Yates if he would like to become a part of the game itself. Dr. Mathlow had created a system called a "Virtual P" that could transfer anyone into the game as the player.

GAME

Entering the game of Spare Balls, which features energy balls, Darius challenges Yates to a duel. Yates agrees. Darius begins to thoroughly blast Yates. Due to his lack of skills, Yates is unable to defend himself from the attacks.

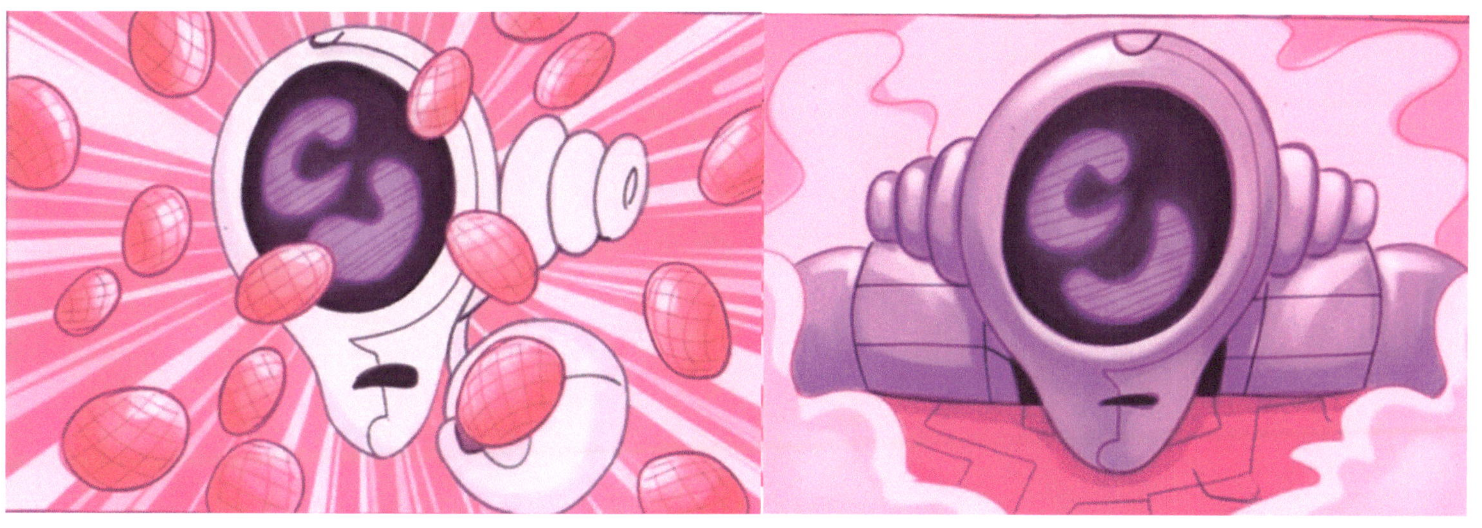

Darius begins to mock him as a failed excuse of a robot. Yates angrily stands up and points his hand in the air. Charging up his energy, he manages to create a purplish-red atom. To both robots' surprise, they detect that Yates's atom is considered hazardous. Darius ignores Rile's pleading to prevent Yates from shooting his spare ball. However, Darius is interested to see just how strong Yates truly is.

Yates hurls the spare ball to him, unruffled by the approaching atom. He uses his one arm as a shield, holding back the blast from the scuffle. This high energy causes an explosion. Both Rile and Yates run to his aid, finding him lying down unconscious.

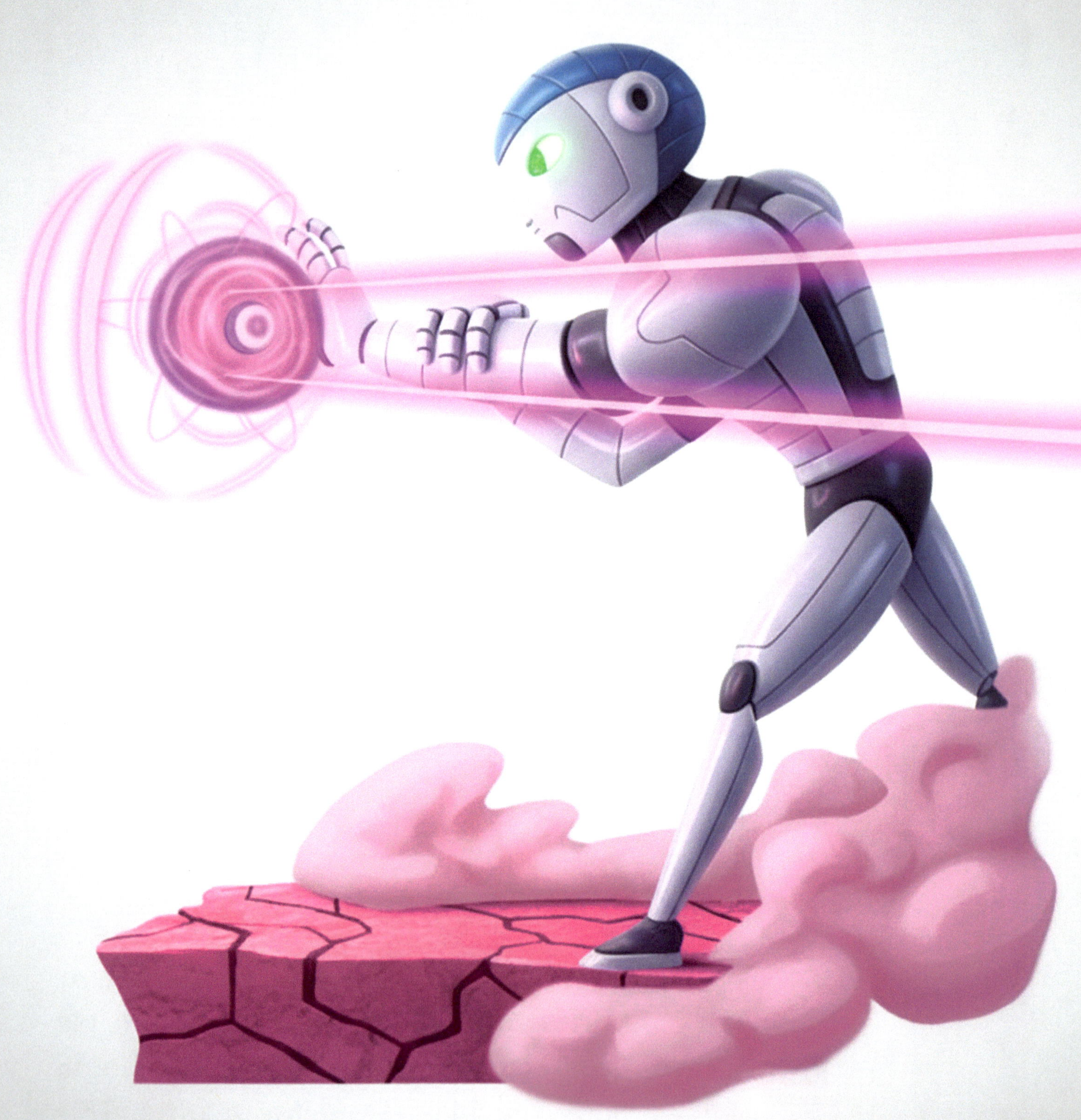

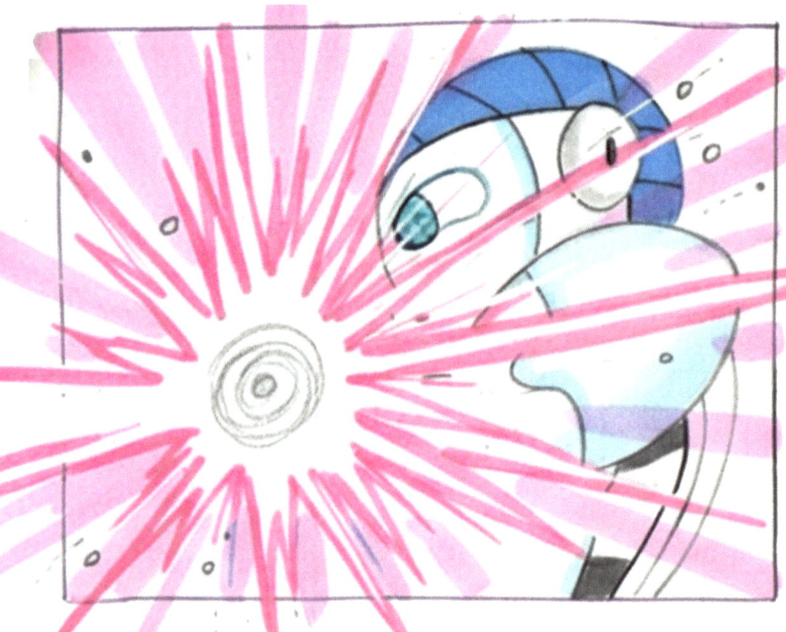

Sometime that same evening, Darius regains consciousness. Rile, Dr. Mathlow, and Yates are all relieved. Darius notices, however, that he has lost his arm. Dr. Mathlow will have to repair him. To their surprise, Yates apologizes for shattering his arm. Darius affirms it was his fault for being arrogant of the way he acted toward Yates.

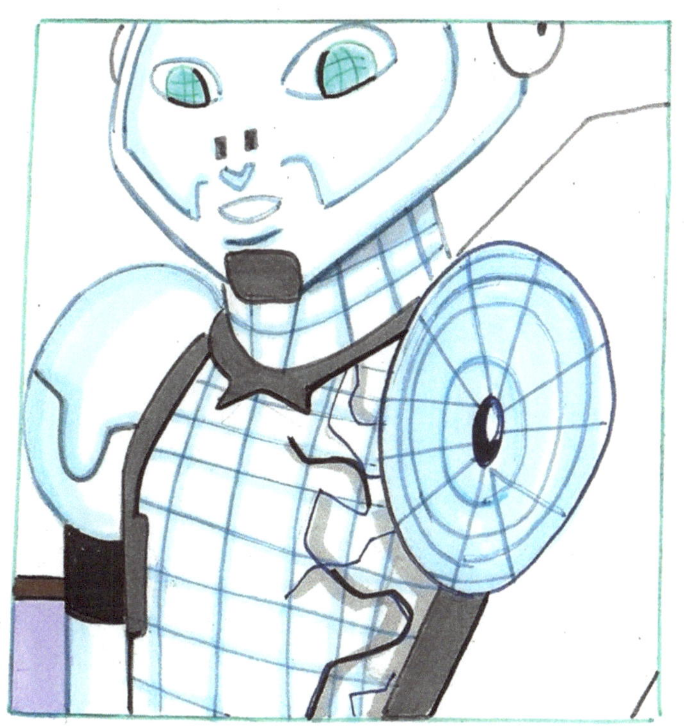

While both fist-bump, they begin to bond over their brotherhood. Both Dr. Mathlow and Rile become delighted. They are now a family under one roof.

ACT 111

Deep out in the void of the universe, a young lady, Tamera, is in the realm of a Dignity named Knowledge, who sees all and knows all, granting wishes to anyone residing on the planet Fitz. After landing her spacecraft, Tamera makes her way up the staircase toward his temple.

Upon arriving, she notices a mysterious vase in which Knowledge comes out of. A large floating creature with a visible brain, two eyes on both sides and squid tentacles, Knowledge proceeds to ask why she has come all this way.

She responds, "I have a question that I must ask. It's urgent." Knowledge informs her that she must first defeat her opponent before he grants her wish. Accepting the challenge, she is introduced to Triple Shredder, a giant orange monster with three layers of teeth.

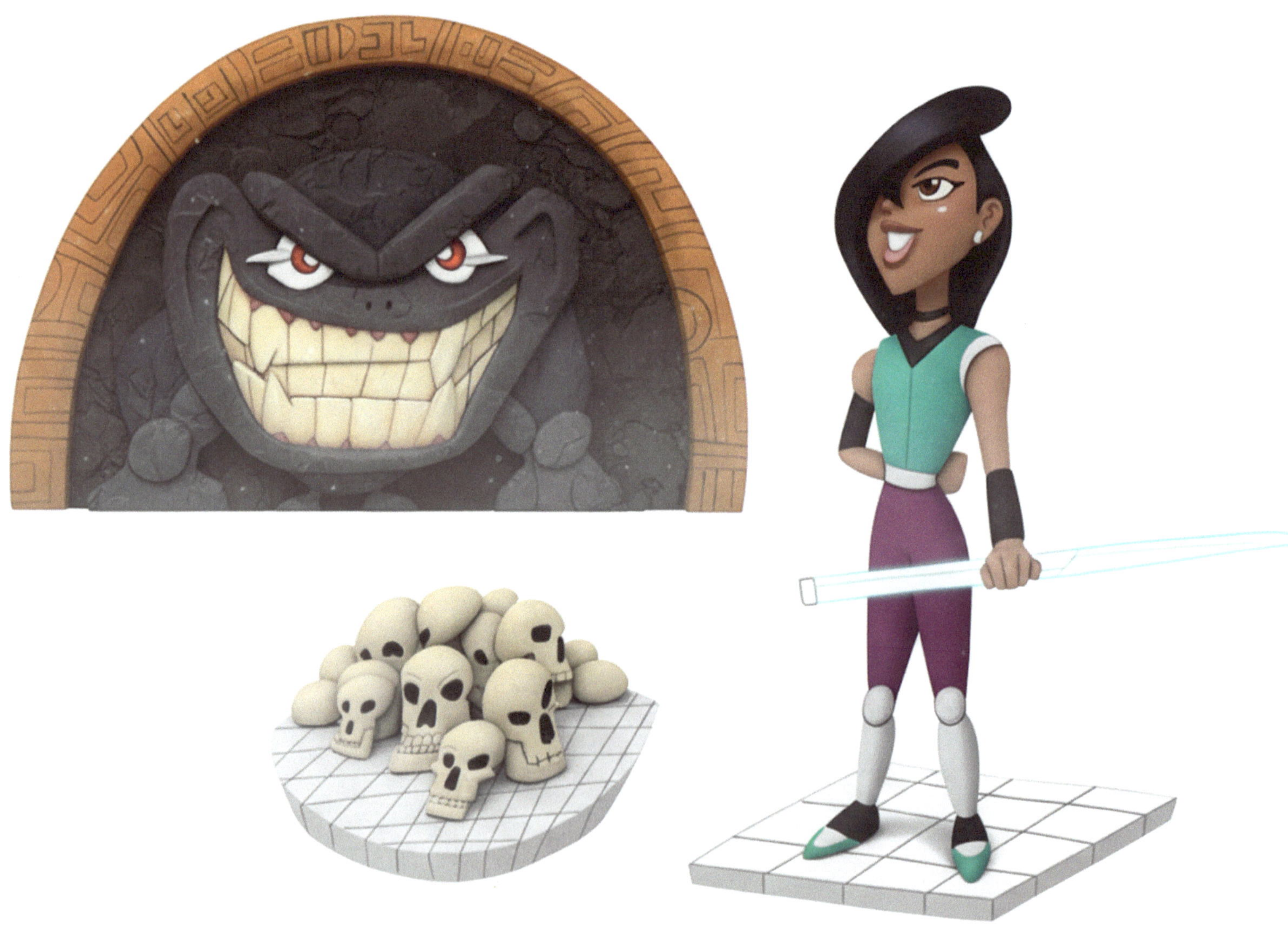

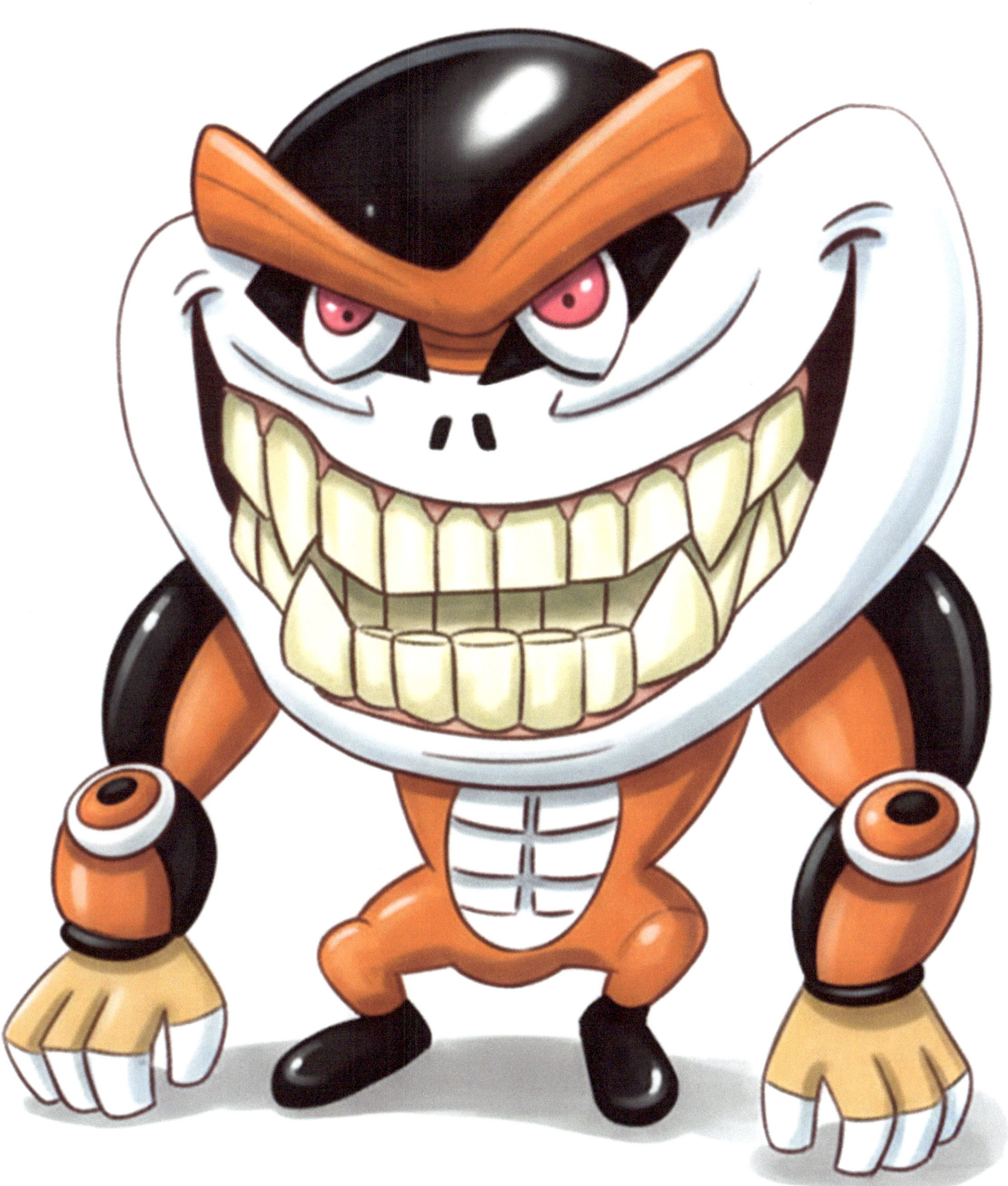

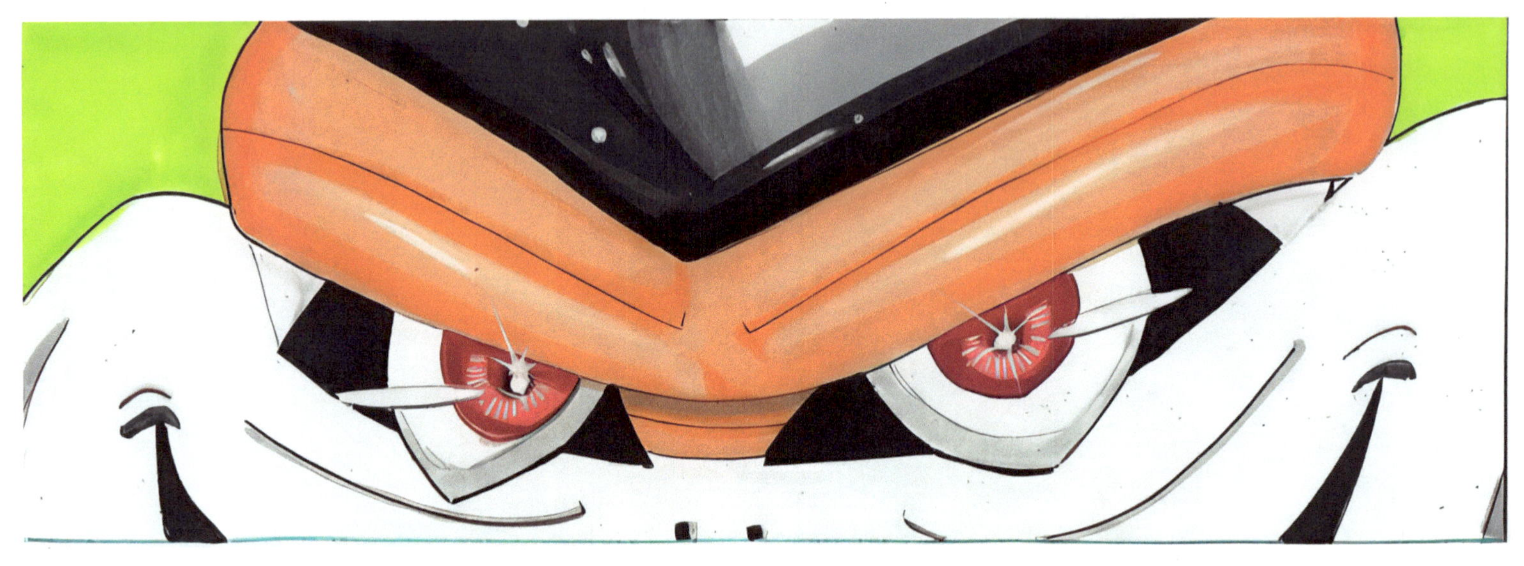

As both battle, Tamera shows to be a very skillful fighter, managing to take down Triple Shredder with her extended pole. Impressed by her fighting skills and determination, Knowledge agrees to grant her wish.

However, before doing so, he would like to learn more about Tamera. Instead of Tamera telling him about her life, he views her memories leading up her visit.

The memory goes back to Earth in 2095, where a city is in ruins. A mutant monkey is searching through the ruins to find survivors to eliminate. Suddenly the monkey hears a cry from the distance. Inside a van is an eight-year-old Tamera holding what appears to be a doll, finally able to stop her cries.

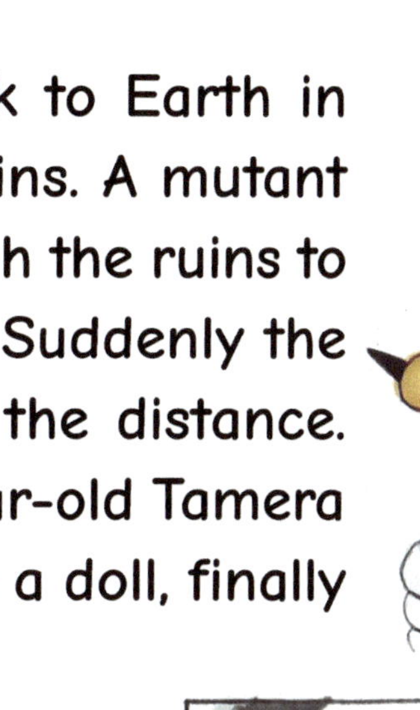

Tamera looks through the window. The monkey seems to be gone till he jumps onto the car window. Frightening her, the monkey proceeds to pull off the car roof to reach her. The monkey begins to pull Tamera by her hair as she screams loudly for help.

Just then, a man in a robotic suit shoots the monkey. Tamera is rescued, and the man in suit signals for his Space Copter as they board it. Turning around, he notices the same monkey has survived the blast and is now back with his laser gun. The man in the suited armor finishes him off for good with one triggered grenade.

On board the craft, the soldier assures Tamera that the Regional Society will protect and care for her. Saddened, Tamera is comforted by her baby sister, who was thought to have been a baby doll. Reassured they will still have each other, they embrace in a loving hug together as they fly away from Earth.

Eight years later, Tamera has joined allegiance to the Regional Society. Shown to be an excellent candidate, she is finally qualified for a higher ranking. She is appointed to explore the galaxy, hoping to retrieve secrets on their adversaries in regard to Battle Against Worlds. Congratulated by her peers, she would commence on her mission next month and be away for a whole year.

Finished with her memories, Knowledge begins noticing her nightmares too. Apparently, Tamera and her sister became separated and she has been desperately searching for her whereabouts since. Knowledge tells Tamera that she holds a purpose beyond what she initially believed in.

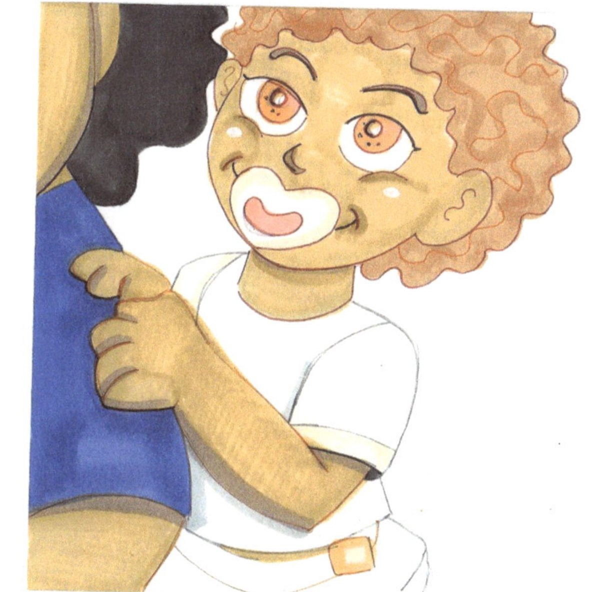

He says she will eventually rejoin with her sister. He sends her off to the next destination, the location of the planet Solar Moon.

Appreciative in her quest, she leaves, excited to see her sister again. Hovering into the galaxy, Tamera decides to take a nap as it will take approximately forty-five days before she arrives on Solar. She disguises the spacecraft as a star. That way, it will be unnoticeable to space troopers, keeping her from being detained for trespassing. Tamera then falls asleep, holding tight a photograph of both siblings.

ARC IV

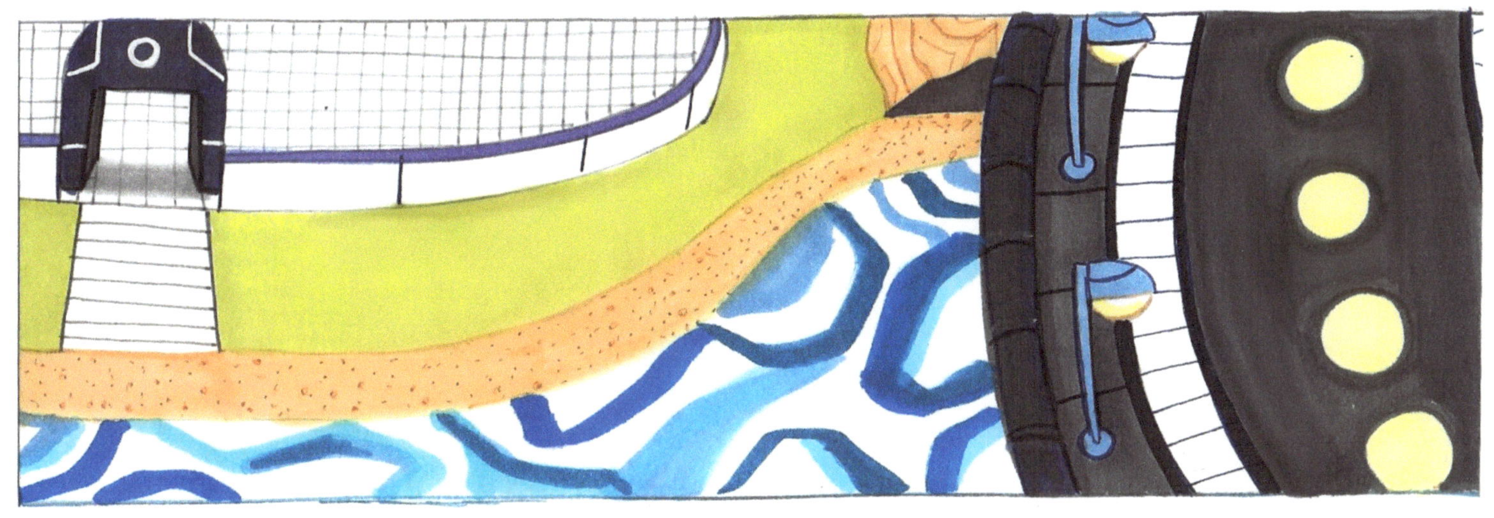

Zion and Scratch are both down at a waterfront. Scratch is seen to be standing in the water fishing.

Scratch says, "Hey, I think I finally caught one!"

As he pulls in his fishing line, the fish leaps out of the water. Both Scratch and the fish scuffle with each other until Scratch loses grip of his fishing pole.

Scratch yells, "There goes my lunch!"

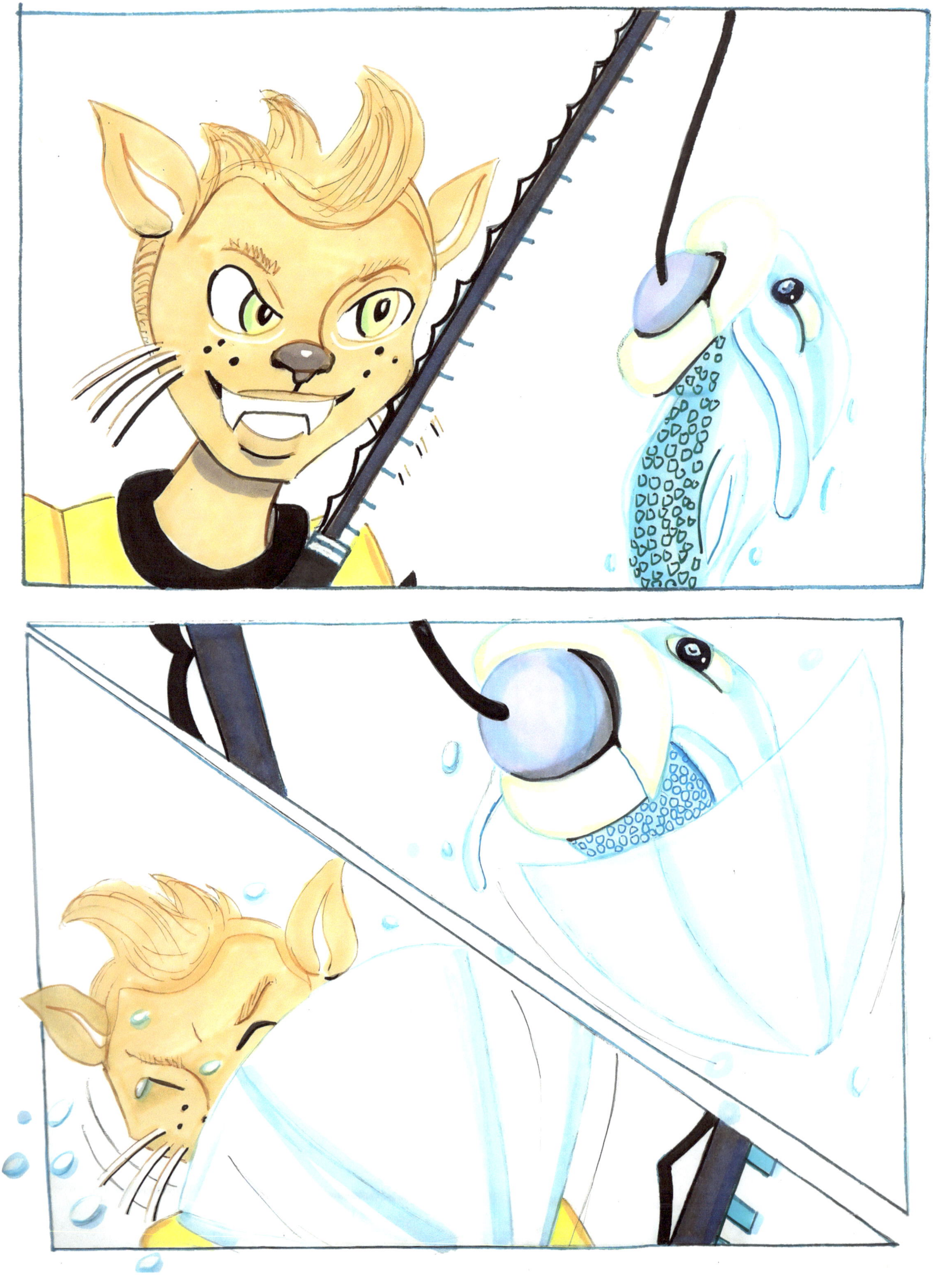

Scratch lowers his face into the water, only for the fish to leap out, splashing water into his face.

Zion finds this amusing while the fish swims away. "Come on, bro! I would've caught him easily."

Annoyed, Scratch tells him, "Yeah, all right. We'll just see about that."

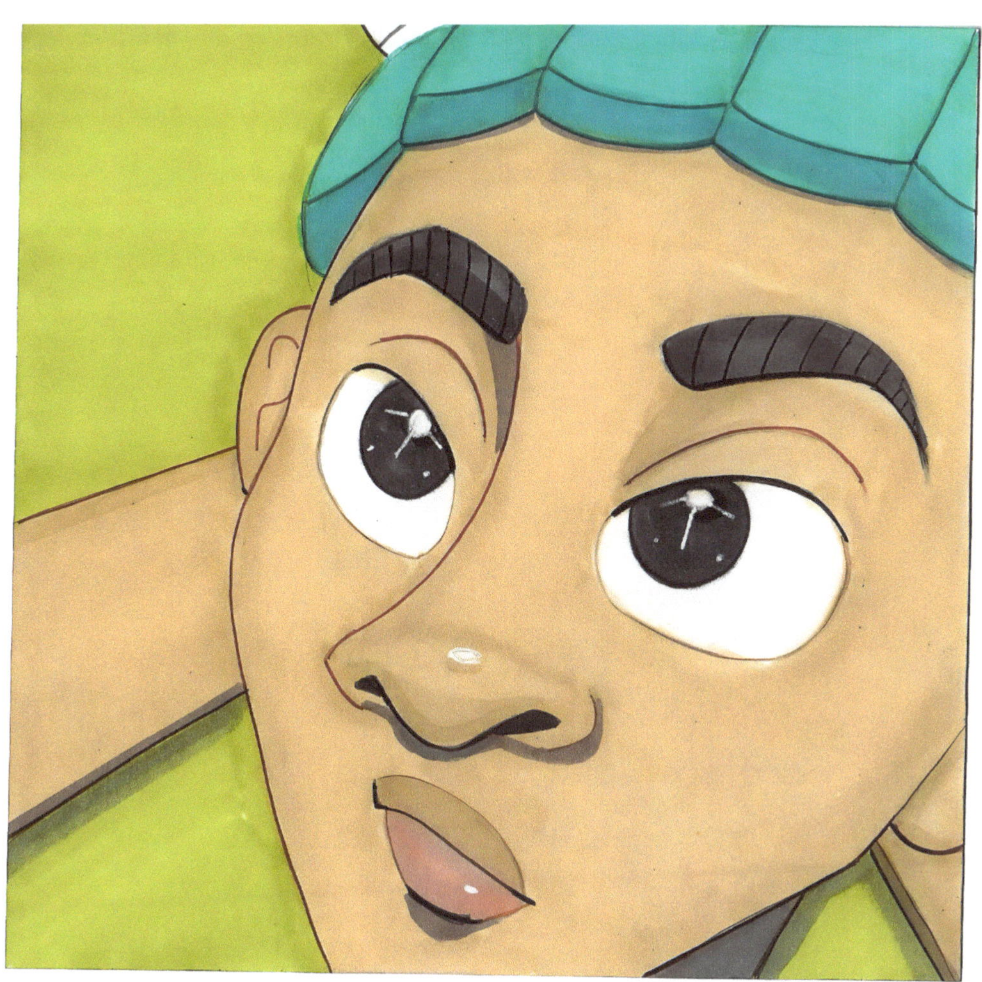

Scratch continues his fishing, while Zion admires the sky view. He notices a mysterious star he has never seen before.

Zion says, "Scratch, look above in the distance. You see what I see?"

The star's faraway twinkling amazes Scratch.

Zion adds, "I've never seen anything like it before."

Scratch replies, "Maybe it's a comet?"

"Maybe," states Zion. "But I don't believe so."

They stare at the mysterious star. Their friend Ebony is heard shouting their names. "Zion and Scratch!"

Zion says, "Hey, what's up, Ebony? Come down here."

Ebony replies, "What are you guys doing here?"

Scratch says, "What does it look like?"

Ebony replies, "I can see that, but why?"

Scratch says, "Fishing, duh!"

Ebony states, "Yeah, Scratch. Perfect excuse to skip school!"

Zion says, "Listen. We're sorry for leaving you behind."

Before he could finish his explanation, Ebony cuts him off. "Honestly you guys are missing out!"

Zion says, "Trust me. Nobody is missing out with Ms. Beetle."

Both boys laugh, only to disappoint Ebony even more.

Ebony says, "You guys are such class acts."

Scratch states, "Who cares? She's so annoying."

Zion agrees, "Exactly. She doesn't like us too."

Ebony says, "That's because you guys keep pulling pranks."

Zion states, "Come on. The last one was harmless."

Ebony reply, "You guys caused her to break three of her limbs."

Scratch laughs hysterically.

Ebony replies, "You guys will never learn."

Zion says, "We promise to make it right, okay? Right, Scratch?"

Scratch, shrieking, is detained by an octopus and confronted by a mutant fish accompanied by the same fish from earlier. They both begin to pummel Scratch.

Zion points Ebony to where the mysterious star is. "Look at that."

Ebony says, "It's beautiful."

Zion replies, "It's been there for at least an hour now."

Ebony says, "I wonder what it is."

After being beaten up, the little fish knocks Scratch out of the water. He joins Zion and Ebony looking at the distant star.

Scratch asks, "Hey, Zion. Do you still think about your father?"
"Of course, I do. Every day. He's out there somewhere."
Ebony asks, "What happened to him?"
"He joined the army to aid the war against worlds. Mom and I haven't heard or seen him in over five years."

Scratch says, "That long, bro?"

"Yeah. He could be dead, and we wouldn't even know it. The service hasn't been helpful in telling us about him or anything." The absence of his father in his life saddens him.

Ebony places her hand onto Zion, providing a warm heart for his sorrow. "He'll be back. Just you wait and see."

Scratch says, "She's right. He's probably closer to us in a shuttle, returning home now."

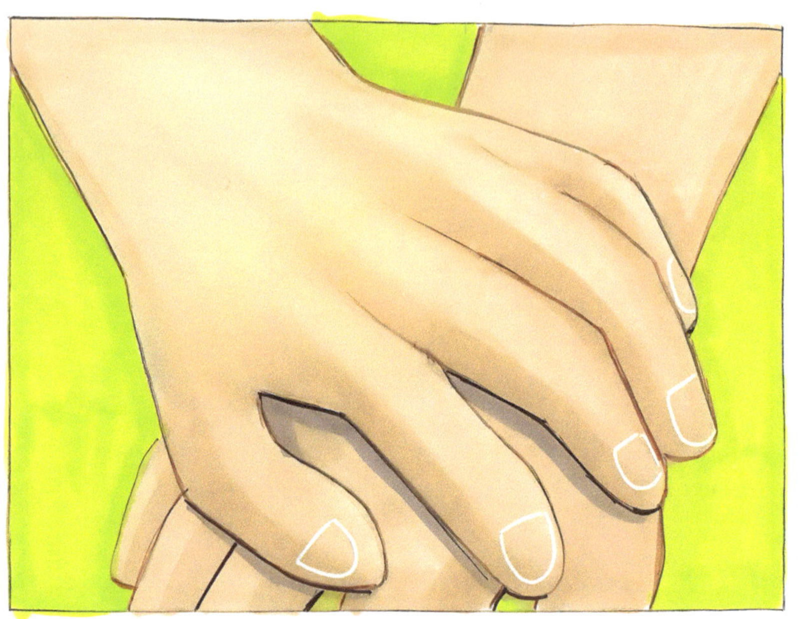

Tyreese, a lion hybrid creeping behind a bush, springs out, clutching Ebony into his arms. He is pleading that she rekindle their relationship. "C'mon, Ebony. Be mine again."

Ebony yells, "No! We are through."

Tyreese argues, "You don't understand. I—"

Ebony says, "You had your chances and blew them!"

Tyreese states, "Let me guess. You love one of these fools?"

Ebony says, "These guys are my friends!"

Scratch whispers to Zion, "Man, is he desperate or nah?" Zion chuckles.

Tyreese says, "I heard that, kitty cat. You think you're a tough guy, huh. Well, do you?"

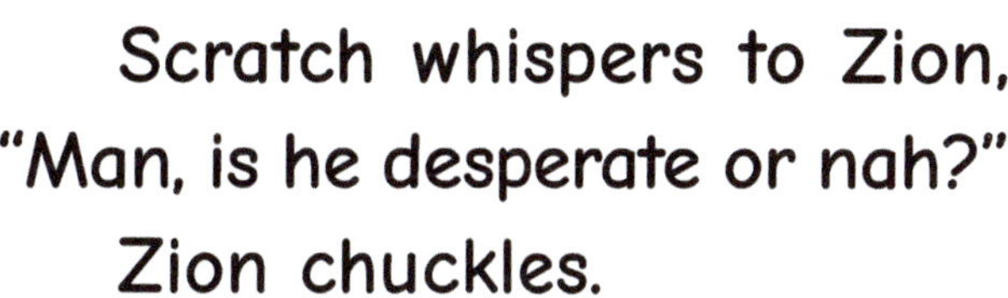

Zion replies, "Calm down, Ebony is our friend. She doesn't want you. Just accept it, bro, and move along."

Tyreese asks, "Is that so?"

Zion says, "Clearly you're not fit for her with your wildest nature for prey."

Tyreese gazes menacingly at Zion while his stomach begins to growl loudly. "So you're the reason she dumped me."

Ebony tells him, "He was not involved in this."

Tyreese growls, "No more excuses."

Ebony asks, "What excuses?"

Tyreese tells them, "You know what I like?"

Zion says, "Huh?"

Tyreese proclaims, "You! I like you, prey!" Tyreese violently tries to attack Zion.

Scratch yells, "Run, bro! Run!"

Ebony exclaims, "Hurry! Get out of here!"

Zion yells, "Ah!"

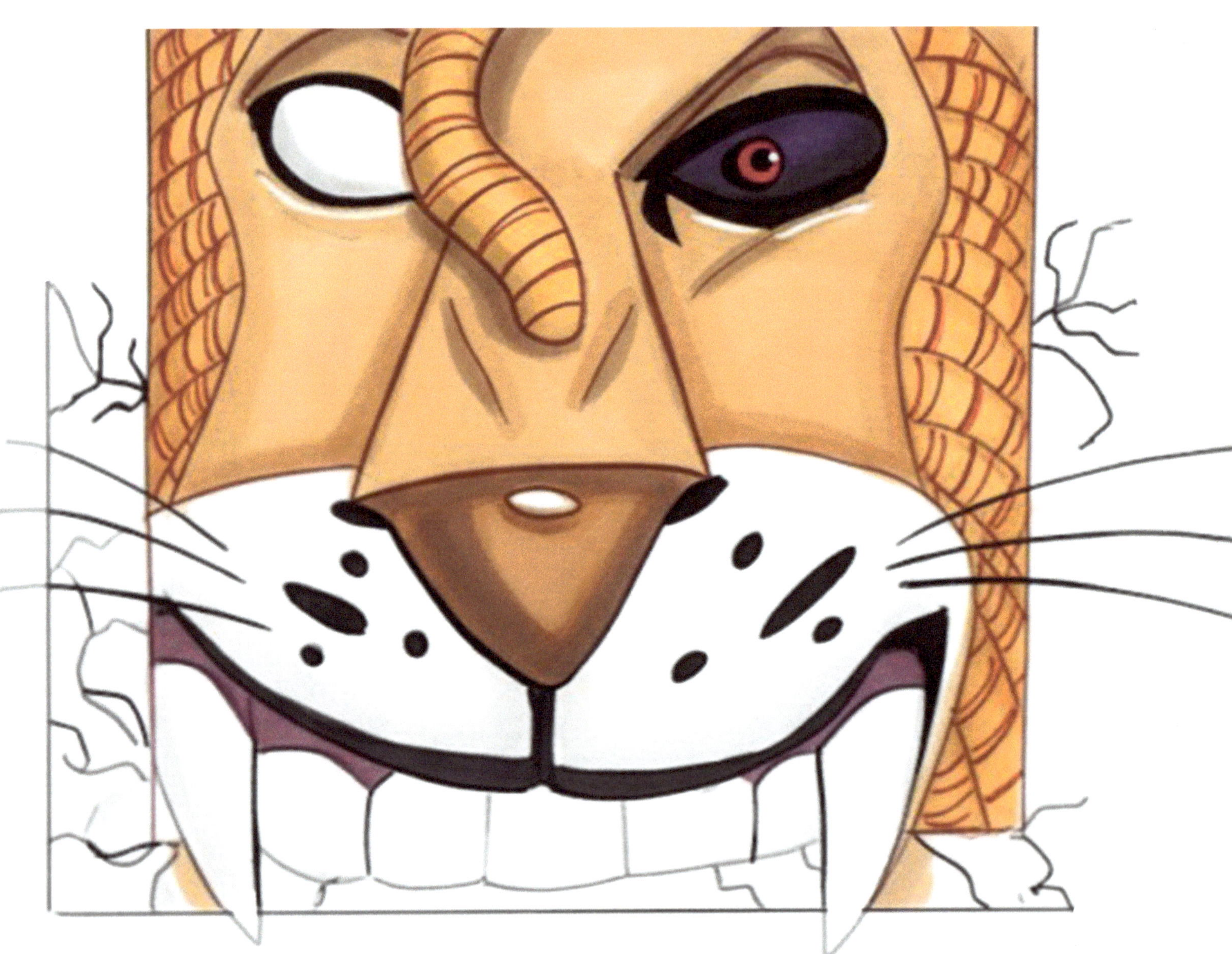

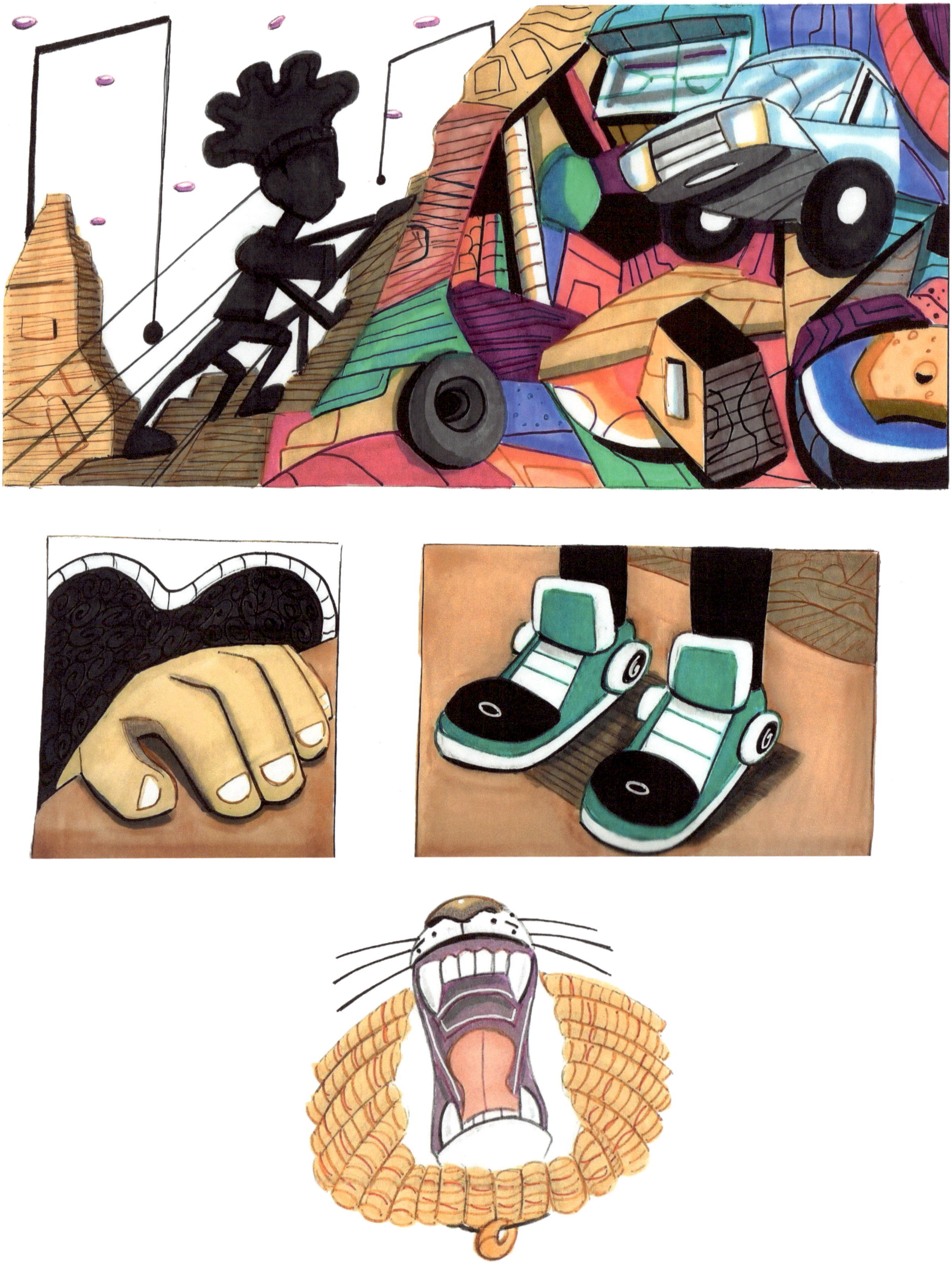

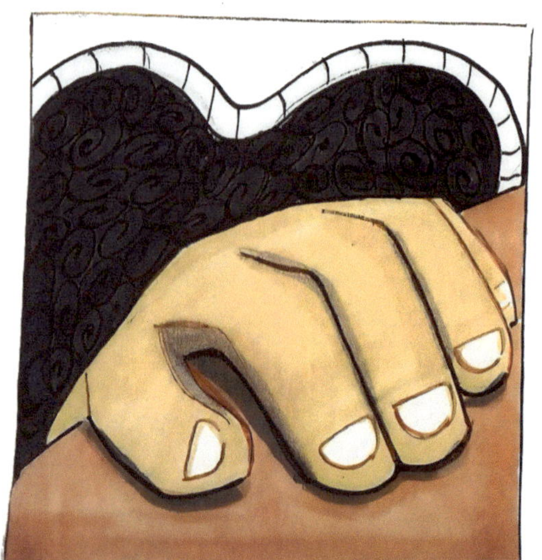

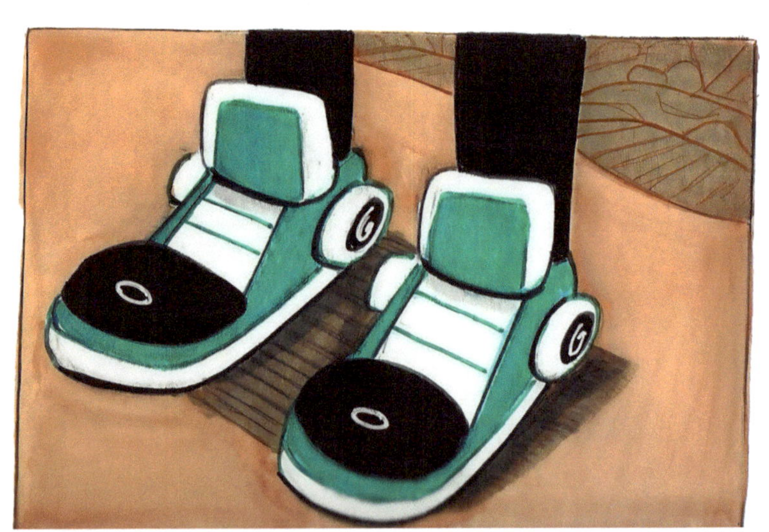

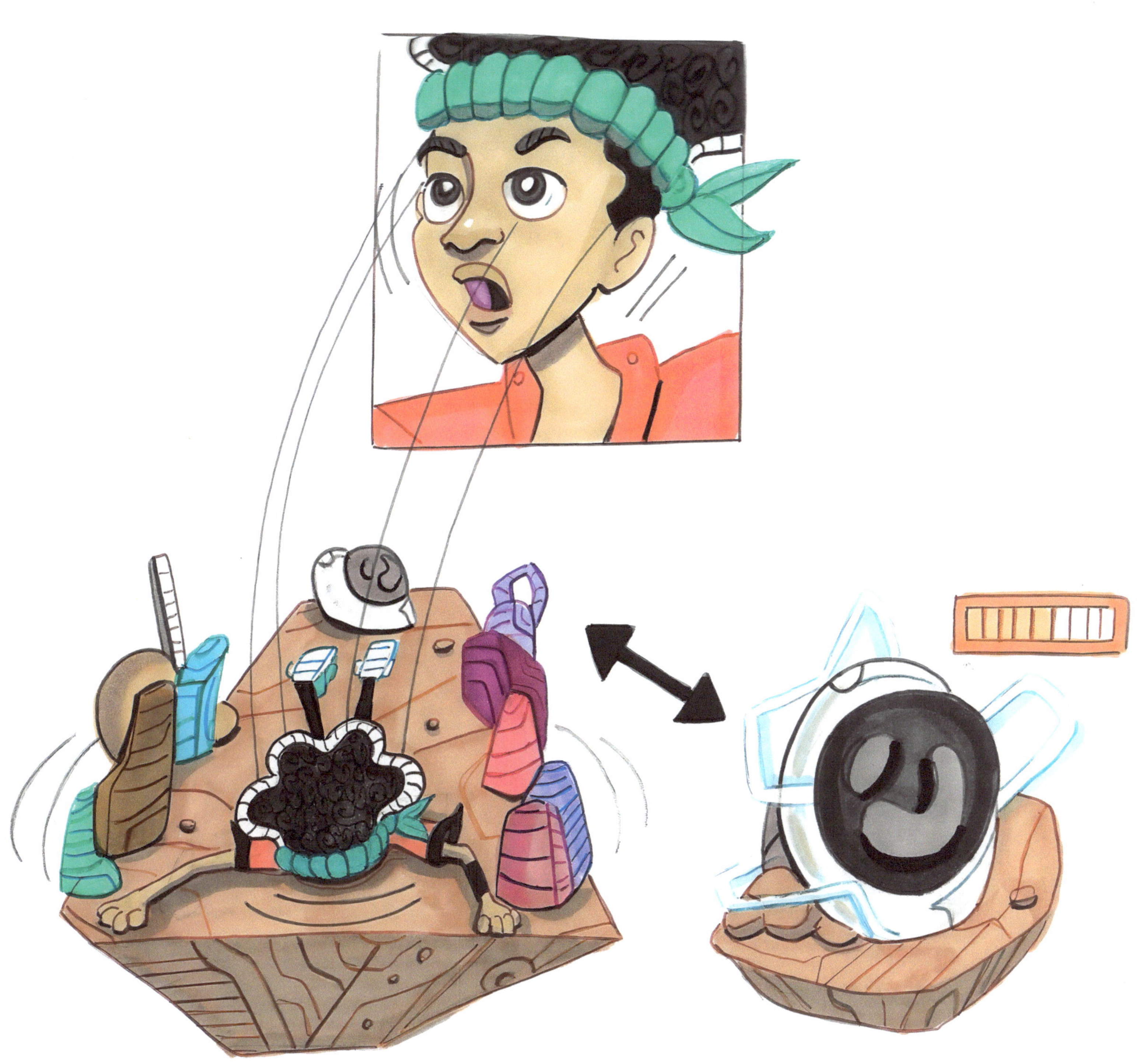

Chased by Tyreese, Zion runs into the open gates of the junkyard. Climbing up piles of junk and space cars, he safely loses Tyreese until he stumbles across a deactivated Yates.

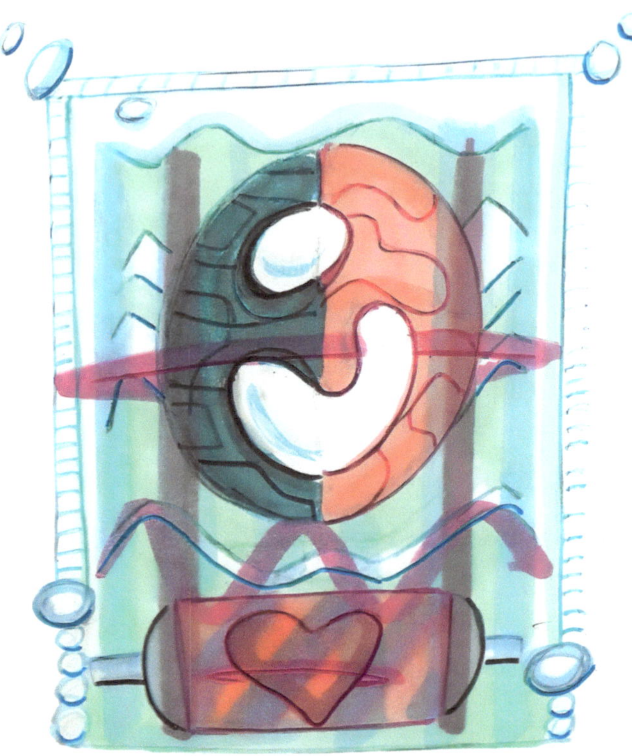

Yates begins reprogramming. "Activating Unit 22.5 Yates. Yates." Yates then walks up to a motionless Zion while scanning the area of its whereabouts. "Location 245. Sinister junkyard, 07206 Solar."

Zion asks, "What are you?"

"Hi. My name is Yates."

"Yates? My name is Zion."

Yates asks, "Would you like to play spare ball with me?"

Zion answers back, "Aren't you a robot?"

Yates replies, "No, a cyborg. I am part-human."

"Really," says Zion. "So what are you doing here?"

Yates replies, "I can't remember."

Zion says, "I mean, you must have an inventor or somewhere you belong." He sees damage on Yates. "You're damaged from behind."

"I will need to be repaired," Yates tell him.

Zion replies, "I don't know any scientist. Maybe Mom can help you out."

Yates asks, "Is she a scientist?"

"No. But my mother is a wise woman. She probably could get you fixed up."

Yates asks, "Can I also stay with you?"

Zion replies, "Sure thing!"

"Thanks," says Yates. "I hate being alone."

Zion tells him, "Don't worry. You'll be safe with me around."

Tyreese is on top of a mountain pile of junk and roars. "Prey! Oh, prey! I'm coming for you!"

Zion, frightened, cries, "I nearly forgot about him!"

Yates asks, "A friend of yours?"

"No," replies Zion. "He's after me."

Both starts running.

Yates tells him, "Maybe I can help you."

Zion says, "Are you sure? You're in bad shape."

Yates replies, "Yes. My jet wings are still functional."

Zion: "All right. Fly us out of here."

Yates exclaims, "Grab onto me."

Yates piggybacks Zion as Tyreese runs closer. Yates's jet wings spread out and blasts both into the air, flying out of the junkyard.

Zion laughs. "Aye, Tyreese. Better luck next time!"
Tyreese roars. "This isn't over, prey!"
Zion says, "That was a close one. Thank you, Yates."

Soaring in the sky, Zion sights the star again. This time, it's a spacecraft landing on a nearby island.

Zion says, "That's the star from earlier. It's a spaceship."

Yates replies, "It looks like it's landing on that island over there."

Zion exclaims, "My father! It might be him. He's returned. Yates, take us over there. We need to check out that spacecraft."

"Hold on."

As they approach the island, they see the ship landing near the mountains.

"Over there, Yates. Let's get closer."
Yates sends out an alarm. "Alert! Alert! Fuel tank is low."
Zion says, "You must be kidding me."
Yates says, "We're going down. Brace for impact!"

"Aaaahhhhhh!" screams Zion.

Both crash-land into the jungle.

Yates says, "Are you okay, Zion?"

"I'll live to see the next day. We need to find that ship."

Yates states, "Before we crashed, my sensors indicated we're not far from its landing."

"Where is it?" asks Zion.

Yates replies, "About twenty-five minutes away from here, to our left side of the mountain."

"Great," says Zion. "Let's go check it out."

Finding the spacecraft, Zion notices the ship isn't of the planet's property. "This spacecraft doesn't look of the army or refugees."

Yates replies, "Maybe he had to use this vehicle to get back here."

Zion asks, "Did you hear that?"

Just then, the doors slowly open with a bright light.

Yates says, "Something or someone is coming out."

Both stare upon a mysterious being, which is revealed to be a girl.

Tamera exclaims, "I've finally made it. It took me some time, but I'm here. I won't leave this planet till I find you."

Spotting Zion and Yates, she leaps down toward them. "Hello. My name is Tamera. I am from the Regional Society."

"How are you? My name is Zion, and this here is Yates."

Yates says, "Hello. Would you like to play spare ball?"

Tamera replies, "How cute are you!"

Zion asks, "Question."

Tamera replies, "Yes?"

Zion says, "You're from Regional. Do you have anyone else on board?"

"Just me. This is my spacecraft." She made it invisible to the eye disguised as a star.

Zion speaks sadly, "Oh . . ."

"Is this the planet Solar?"

"Yes," says Zion. "Are you a tourist?"

"No. My sister and I became estranged in outer space. I've been searching for her. I was told she might had landed on this very planet."

"Not sure," says Zion. "You would have to search for her in Solar City."

Yates says, "There's something coming."

Tamera asks, "Where?"

Unexpectedly, law enforcement apprehends them using a light beam that hovers them into the airship. They are handcuffed, and Yates is sealed into an electrical cube.

Yates asks, "Are we in trouble, Zion?"

Zion says, "Hey, what's going on? We didn't do anything!"

Officer 99.7 exclaims, "Silence! You punks broke Lord Spice's Law 253 that forbids outsiders without proper identification onto this planet, usage of an artificial being, and trespassing on this island."

Zion tells him, "We're just kids. Give us a break."

Officer 99.7 replies, "Yeah, kids who love to skip school."

Officer 99.7 adds, "We will be heading into Solar City. You three are to be detained for questioning and face your judgment.

Zion concludes, "This is not how I planned my day. Mom is going to kill me for this."

Special Thanks,

Kevin Santiago Heydi Perez

Christian Huguley Sunny DeSouza

Isaiah McClain Theresa Lee Kyle Lee Doris Santos

Victoria Wiafe Taya Nicole Davis Jada Locklear Tre'Son Birotte

Lauren Pancurak Yeats Raquel Garcia John Badiola Eliana Jumbo

John Branco Essence Austion Samuel Covington Dondre Jackson

Tyreese Wise Essence Kelly Derrick Austin Derrick Lee Devin Lee

Garette Carlyle Thompson Joven Rosales Denise Lee Lamont Lee

Ski Sharif Howard Julius Lee Mary Helen Lee Christopher Keil

Al-Rahmier Rushon Johnson Unie Thomas Daney Adams

Anthony Nicoli Joseph Hill Darlin Barthleus

Nicholas Lopez

Special Thanks,

Kevin Santiago Heydi Perez

Christian Huguley Sunny DeSouza

Isaiah McClain Theresa Lee Kyle Lee Doris Santos

Victoria Wiafe Taya Nicole Davis Jada Locklear Tre'Son Birotte

Lauren Pancurak Yeats Raquel Garcia John Badiola Eliana Jumbo

John Branco Essence Austion Samuel Covington Dondre Jackson

Tyreese Wise Essence Kelly Derrick Austin Derrick Lee Devin Lee

Garette Carlyle Thompson Joven Rosales Denise Lee Lamont Lee

Ski Sharif Howard Julius Lee Mary Helen Lee Christopher Keil

Al-Rahmier Rushon Johnson Unie Thomas Daney Adams

Anthony Nicoli Joseph Hill Darlin Barthleus

Nicholas Lopez

www.ingramcontent.com/pod-product-compliance
Lightning Source LLC
Chambersburg PA
CBHW041126100726
47911CB00002B/52